LOUTH

FOLK
TALES

LOUTH

FOLK TALES

DOREEN MCBRIDE

The History Press Ireland

First published 2015

The History Press Ireland
50 City Quay
Dublin 2
Ireland
www.thehistorypress.ie

British Library Cataloguing in Publication Data.
A catalogue record for this book is available from the British Library.

ISBN 978 1 84588 848 0

Typesetting and origination by The History Press
Printed and bound in Great Britain by TJ International Ld.

CONTENTS

ACKNOWLEDGEMENTS

Thanks are due to my wee Granny Henry, Auntie Carrie and Auntie Teenie, who flooded my mind with stories when I was a child. They have given me a legacy for which I am eternally grateful. Thanks are also due to: students in my classes both in the Department of Continuing Education, Queen's University Belfast and the University of Ulster; people I met on the road, especially Sister Betty; Dr Tim Campbell, Director of the Saint Patrick's Centre, Downpatrick for information about St Patrick; Dr Jonathan Bell, Ulster Folk and Transport Museum, Cultra, for information on folklore; Peter Carr, White Row Press, for information on the 'Big Wind'; Betty Quinn, Brendan Matthews and the staff at Drogheda Museum, Millmount, Drogheda, for inspiration, information about Oliver Cromwell and some great tales; Paddy Rispin, local historian, Trim, for the gory details regarding medieval justice; Canon Sean O'Doherty for information on St Brigid; Dara Vallely, one of the Armagh Rhymers, who is a font of knowledge regarding pagan practices and for information regarding St Brigid; Larry Breen and J.J. Woods, local historians, for encouragement; Kevin Woods, the Leprechaun Whisperer, Carlingford; the staff of Dundalk Tourist Board, especially Sinead, Steve Lally, Liz Weir, Kate Muldoon, Linda Ballard, the late John Campbell, Mike O'Leary and Francis Quinn, who are great storytellers; Father Quinn, parish priest Louth Village, for information and the time he spent showing me the church and tree at Ardpatrick that are associated with Saint Oliver Plunkett; Sean Collins, lecturer, tourist guide and local historian; the late Joan Gaffney for the story about Lassara's Leap; Crawford Howard for permission to print his comic verse, 'Saint Patrick and the Snakes'; the staff of the Linen Hall Library; the staff of Banbridge Library; Hector McDonnell, author and local historian; the late Ernest Scott for some great yarns, and a mountain of craic; the late Dr Jack Doyle, Senior Lecturer of English Literature, Sumter Campus, University of South Carolina; the late Archbishop Otto Simms, Armagh, for spending a day enthusing me about Celtic culture; the late Revd Eric Gallagher, past president of the Methodist Church in Ireland, who was the first to tell me the story about St Patrick and the shamrock; Tom McDevitte, alias Barney McCoo, for passing his stories on to me and spending time taking me to the relevant places; Roisin Cox for the story about Willy John's Big Surprise; Dr Jim Mallory, Queen's University, Belfast, for information regarding life in the Iron Age; Dr Kay Muir, Queen's University, Belfast, for information pertaining to the Ulster Cycle of Tales; and finally to my cousin Vernon Finlay.

INTRODUCTION

One of my earliest memories is of being taken by my parents to the tiny two-up two-down house on Belfast's Shankill Road, where my great-grandmother, Martha Henry, lived. We were greeted by old Granny's youngest daughter, Auntie Teenie, who came to the door in a great state of excitement.

'Mother,' she said, 'says if we're good childer, she'll tell us a story.'

'Stuff and nonsense,' Dad snorted, 'I'm away to see Jim,' and with that, he disappeared to visit his cousin, who lived further down the street.

Neighbours crowded into the tiny room, which became full to overflowing. We had a memorable evening. I'll never forget the sight of Old Granny sitting in a stick-back chair, her gentle, melodic voice, the gleam of her silver hair and the way her hands moved gracefully in the firelight to emphasise important points. I can't remember the gist of the story, just something about a king, a queen, a knave and silver.

The question is, was Dad right to dismiss storytelling as a 'waste of time'? I think he was wrong for the following reasons.

On a simple, basic level, storytelling helps develop appreciation of the past and a closer relationship between adults and children. It counteracts the 'instant' culture in which we live. Storytelling improves powers of concentration, develops the imagination and sensitivity as the ability to empathise with characters develops.

It is possible to teach morality through story without appearing to preach, and to allow dreams and subconscious fears to surface and be expressed in a safe environment. Storytelling is central to literature, and it is worth mentioning that Ireland, which is a nation of storytellers, has five writers who have won Nobel Prizes for English Literature.

I was blessed because my father's mother and her sisters were gifted storytellers. Granny Henry told traditional Irish stories.

Aunt Teenie had her own twist on well-loved tales such as Little Red Riding Hood and Cinderella. She acted out the big bad wolf and the ugly sisters and had us in kinks of laughter. Auntie Carrie, meanwhile, told outrageous stories about family history, arousing in me a lifelong interest in folklore and local history. Through her I learnt about employment in a linen mill and the fun workers had singing songs together such as 'The Tidy Doffer', how they played tricks on each other, and the dangers inherent in their work.

Auntie Carrie gave an insight into social customs and folklore of the Edwardian age. She described how one Sunday, dressed in her best, she joined her friends walking up the Antrim Road in Belfast. The girls hoped to meet 'good-looking fellas'. Unfortunately, she had severe bowel problems en route. She described – with sound effects – the disastrous consequences as she ran towards home, providing my family with happy memories of the companionship engendered by mutual laughter.

During my work as an international storyteller I was frequently astounded by the effect of story on adult audiences. Individuals often made comments, such as 'that transported me back to my childhood', and 'I don't know why but I found that story very healing' and 'I now have a greater appreciation of what my ancestors' life was like'.

As a child, my favourite story was Cinderella. In retrospect, I think I loved that story because it expressed the possibility of escape from unhappy circumstances. My father was what is now referred to as bipolar. Terrible bouts of depression alternated with manic high spirits and intervening episodes of normality. I never knew what kind of a mood he was going to be in, how he would react to my presence, or how to please him.

I have observed other children reacting to an old story in unexpected ways. I remember once telling a group of eight-year-olds about the 'Leanhaun Shee', a beautiful, but wicked fairy who, I said, wanted to kiss the boys. Actually she's a fairy mistress, but I wasn't going to tell eight-year-olds that. If they kissed her, she would put an evil spell on them. (I was attempting to tell the class sometimes it is right to say 'No'.) The boys, who were at the age at which they did not like girls, were killing themselves laughing, all except for one poor wee mite. He looked very thoughtful. It was Halloween and the teacher asked me to tell a ghost story. I was about halfway through when the wee mite put his hand up and wistfully asked, 'When will the beautiful woman come for me?'

I could have wept for him.

I love the old traditional tales because they have been honed and edited over centuries and can be trusted. That was demonstrated to me when I was dazzled by stage lights in a theatre on the campus of Rochester University, New York. I started to tell the traditional story 'The Amadan of Dough'. It's about a king's son who was disliked by his stepmother because he was disabled. Halfway through the story, my eyes adapted to the light and I saw, to my horror, a row of people with Down's Syndrome. Briefly I wondered if I should have been telling that story, but I had no option but to continue. At the interval the organiser came to complain. 'Doreen,' she scolded, 'do you think it was sensitive to tell a story about an educationally challenged lad with a row of Down's Syndrome people in the audience?'

Before I could reply something tugged my skirt. I looked down and saw a child with Down's Syndrome.

'Doreen,' he asked, 'do you see my shoes?'

I duly admired them and he commented, 'With these shoes on I could fight and win like the Amadan.' The organiser then apologised.

I suggest you learn some of the old stories, tell them, keep them alive and teach others to love them. It's easy. Simply pick a story and learn the sequence of events. Don't worry about words, just events. Picture what happens in front of your eyes and describe what you see while telling it. Telling a story is much better than reading aloud. It's like taking your feet off the ground and flying.

1

LEPRECHAUNS AND OTHER FAIRIES

I am indebted to two people: a student in one of my folklore classes at the Department of Continuing Education, Queen's University, Belfast, for telling me about leprechauns and O'Hare's spirit grocer in Carlingford; and Kevin Woods, the leprechaun whisperer, who lives in Carlingford, for bringing my knowledge up to date.

In the past, most towns and villages had a single shop that sold everything you could think of. You could buy milk, good home-made country butter, flour, eggs, fruit, vegetables, sewing needles, thread, biscuits, ham, and coffins. Alcohol was freely available and that type of shop was called a spirit grocers. That was before licensing laws spoilt the fun.

Few spirit grocers have survived but there is one in Carlingford – O'Hare's. It is on the corner of 'The Square' and is well worth a visit.

O'Hare's is divided into two parts. The door from the street leads to a shop with a counter and some groceries stored on shelves. The door at the back leads into what could only be described as a pub. It's a great place if you're looking for good Irish craic. It doesn't matter what time you go, you'll always find friendly people sitting round having fun.

The first time I visited O'Hare's, the then owner, P.J. O'Hare, was still alive. He was a large, jolly, round man with a twinkle in his kindly brown eyes who greeted me in a friendly fashion. I caught sight of a glass cabinet sitting in front of the window and was intrigued by the contents: it held a 'leprechaun' suit and a small skeleton head. I asked P.J. about them and this is the story I was told.

One day, several years ago, a farmer's son was feeling depressed so, to lift his spirits, he went for a walk up the road and into the mountains. Suddenly, when he was near the top of the pass, he heard a cry. It sounded like an animal in pain. He was a kindly young fellow, with an interest in livestock, so went into a field and followed the sound. It appeared to come from somewhere in front of him. He followed it, walking, through one field, into another and then into a third.

The cry suddenly stopped. The lad was upset; he thought the animal had fallen unconscious or had died. He searched, but couldn't find anything and, deciding he was wasting his time, he turned and began to retrace his steps. As he reached the gate of one of the fields, he noticed part of the stone wall had fallen down. Animals would be able to escape and he knew how serious that could be. He was a decent lad and not in a hurry, so he decided to mend the breach. He set to work, picking up boulders, judging where they would fit and putting them back in place. He had nearly finished when he noticed a skull and a brown paper parcel sitting in a cavity. The parcel was in a mess, covered in mud and decaying leaves. He picked it up and brought it to P.J. O'Hare.

P.J. said he was very excited by the parcel. It contained a leprechaun suit with four gold coins in one of its pockets. He bought it from the lad, built the case and put the skull on display along with the leprechaun's suit.

I looked P.J. straight in the eye and said it sounded like a tall story to me, a load of baloney. P.J. wanted to know why I thought such a terrible thing.

I replied that the suit was too small to be worn by a leprechaun. Irish fairies are not small dainty things. Leprechauns are a type of Irish fairy and are as big as a child between the ages of two and six years. There are many type of fairy and some are as big as humans. 'You're kidding,' he exclaimed.

'No I'm not. There's a fairy called a Leanhaun Shee, or fairy mistress who appears like a very beautiful woman. She's looking for love. She'll be your slave if you refuse her, but make love to her and you'll become her slave, get thinner and thinner and eventually die. There will be no rest for you, even beyond the grave. You'll end up wandering the earth as a miserable ghost.'

'You're kidding,' P.J. exclaimed again.

'No I'm not. I'm serious.'

'Do you mean to say, if a Leanhaun Shee came in here I couldn't tell her from a normal woman?'

'That's right.'

'And if I made mad passionate love to her, I'd die?'

'Yes. You'd literally be courting death.'

'Would she have any benefits, do anything for me?'

'Yes, I suppose so. She'd inspire you to write beautiful poetry.'

'That'd be great. Could I grow thin,' asked P.J., patting his corpulent tum, 'write beautiful poetry, become rich and famous, like Seamus Heaney, and then get rid of her?'

'I suppose you could, but the only way to get rid of her would be to get her to fall in love with your best friend.'

'Well, I wish she'd come in here,' P.J. replied, 'I'd take advantage of her and worry about the consequences afterwards. I reckon a group of intelligent men could pass her along the line, so to speak. By the time it was your turn again you might be so old you'd be glad to snuff it. Now tell me, are there any other sorts of fairy? Any wee ones that could fit that suit?'

'There are lots of other types of fairy, but they're all too big. It's a take on.'

'No, it's not,' replied P.J. 'It's the genuine article. It was found up Slieve Foy by a very respectable fella. He was a schoolteacher. Schoolteachers don't tell whoppers. Perhaps it belonged to a baby leprechaun, or even one that didn't grow up properly. Maybe it was a dwarf leprechaun's. We have dwarf humans, so why can't leprechauns have dwarfs too?'

I admitted he had a point, but went on to argue that the skull could not belong to a leprechaun because fairies never die. They used to live in Heaven with God and the angels, but they annoyed God to such an extent that He threw them out of heaven and told them to stay on earth until Judgement Day. Then He'd decide if He was going to give them an immortal soul, like humans, or blow them out like puff of smoke.

P.J. looked disappointed to hear the skull couldn't possibly belong to a leprechaun then smiled and said, 'Perhaps the leprechaun had a pet rabbit and he asked it to guard his clothes. For some reason or other he couldn't get back and the rabbit died looking after them.'

I gave up arguing, bought a drink and sat down beside some friendly people who had invited me to join them.

Every time I am near Carlingford I make the effort to go into O'Hare's. The craic is mighty. It has never disappointed, although the leprechaun suit is no longer in a glass case beside the window. It is now framed and hanging on the wall. According to P.J., some eejit came in one day, got drunk, staggered against the case, knocked it over and smashed it to smithereens. Luckily the contents weren't damaged so they were picked up, dusted down and the glass fragments were removed. P.J. had the new case made and hung on the wall. It's safer there.

One fine summer evening I decided to sit at one of the benches behind the pub. Two men and their wives came and joined me. I asked if they believed in fairies. The men said emphatically that anyone who believes in fairies is 'stark, staring mad'. The women – sisters – were annoyed and claimed to have been terrified by a troop of fairies when they were children.

The men laughed and accused them of being imaginative eejits who'd been fooled by changes in the light at dusk.

The women became very angry and told me what had happened. When they were children they used to play on the Yellow Hill outside Drogheda. On this occasion they were having so much fun that they didn't realise how late it was and before they knew it the sun was beginning to set. They became frightened because their mother had warned them never to be near the yellow hill at twilight as fairies come up from the Otherworld and steal human children.

The girls looked up the hill and were alarmed to see a troop of fairies, singing and dancing in the field above them. They turned and ran home as if the Devil himself was after them.

There was a real sense of fear in the women's voices as they recounted their tale and I feel very privileged to have heard it. Elderly folk in Ireland often tell second-hand stories about fairies – 'I know a man/woman who saw the fairies' and so on – but it is very rare to find somebody who says something along the lines of 'I saw …'

The men continued to scoff at their wives' tale, but the women went on to recall a family experience.

They had a brother. He was the only boy in a large family of girls and he was spoilt rotten. Everything he wished for was granted. He was given the best chair at the table, the largest portion of meat, he never had to do any chores and the women waited on him hand and foot. As a result he grew up to be a charming rascal with no sense of responsibility. He refused to hold down a proper job and broke their poor mother's heart by refusing to go to Mass. He laughed at her warnings about fairies and said he did not believe the 'stupid, superstitious nonsense' their mother spouted about religion and fairies.

One Saturday night, he drove over to Ardee to attend a dance. (He always came home late and in a drunken state. Their mother worried something terrible about him.) On this particular night she had gone to bed and was dozing fitfully when she woke with a start and jumped out of bed. She was crying and shivering with fear. She woke the whole household by yelling at the top of her voice.

'Girls! Girls! Get up! Get up! Your brother is in mortal danger. Come on, come on. We've got to pray for him. Get up, go into the parlour. Come on! Hurry up! We've got to get going before it's too late.' She even hauled their father out of bed, while he was grumbling and griping about hysterical women who wouldn't let a poor auld fella sleep in peace.

Their mother marshalled them into the parlour where they spent the whole night praying, and 'darned uncomfortable it was too, being on your knees for such a long time'. They continued their vigil until shortly after first light, when their brother walked in the back door. He was in a terrible state, shivering with fear and cold and he had his jacket on inside out and back to front. The girls' mother burst into tears and made him sit down by the fire and tell them what had happened.

He said he'd driven over to the dance in Ardee because he'd seen a wee girl he fancied and hoped to meet her. Sure enough, she was standing at the back of the hall, chatting to friends when he arrived. He had a few snifters to give him Dutch courage and asked her for a dance. She refused, saying she never had anything to do with a lad who had taken drink. He was terribly upset and decided to drown his sorrows, so drank what he described as 'a skinful'. He was as drunk as a lord when he climbed into his wee Austin 7 to go home.

There wasn't much traffic on the roads in those days and there were no laws banning drinking and driving. He was within a couple of miles of home when his car suddenly stopped beside the gate of a field. He got out and started to fiddle under the bonnet. He couldn't see anything wrong and what with the cold night air and the fact he'd had what he described as 'a skinful of drink', he had to do what a man has to do. He was a modest sort of a bloke, so opened the gate and went into the field. When he'd relieved himself, he turned to go home and, what do you know? He couldn't find the gate. He walked round and round the field. It didn't have a gate. He thought he was just being stupid because he was one over the eight. Perhaps he'd been staggering around the field at random and had simply missed seeing the exit? He decided to be sensible and conduct a scientific experiment. He took a handkerchief out of his pocket, tied it to the hedge then walked all round the field, staying close to the boundary. He found his handkerchief again but no gate. At that point he remembered what his mother had told him about fairies and was terrified. 'There's nothing like a good dose of fear to make a drunk man sober,' he said.

Their mother had said that fairies lure people they want to steal into fields and cause the gate to disappear. He was panic-stricken. He recalled that they don't like ugly people so, to make himself look as unattractive as possible, he took his jacket off, turned it inside out and put it on back to front.

Fairies do not like humans with food in their stomachs. Luckily, he had half a bar of chocolate in his overcoat pocket. He took it out and began to eat, very slowly, making it last as long as possible. At this point in his story he burst into tears and hugged their mother.

'Mother,' he said, 'thank you. I'd have been stolen if it hadn't been for you. I'd have been doomed. Doomed. I'd never have seen you again.'

He'd spent the night praying as he walked around the field looking for the gate. It didn't reappear until dawn. He opened it and went back to his car, which started without any problem and he drove home. He said he was a changed man. And he was. He no longer scoffed at his mother's beliefs. He went to Mass every week, stopped drinking and gambling, got himself a good steady job and became a pillar of society. He's now on the local council and works hard to support his wife and growing family.

'What about the wee girl he fancied in the dance hall at Ardee?' I asked.

One of the sisters laughed. 'Aye,' she said, 'my brother doesn't give up easily. He went back, stayed stone cold sober and asked her to dance. She looked a bit doubtful but he told her he was a changed man and pleaded for her to give him a chance. The upshot was they've been married for years. She's a great wee wife and they have four children with another on the way'.

Years after P.J. O'Hare died, I met Kevin Woods, the leprechaun whisperer. He told me he was once walking around his garden when he saw something glinting on the wall. He investigated and found four pieces of leprechaun gold. He knew within his heart that the leprechauns were trying to contact him so immediately climbed up Slieve Foy, the mountain that towers over Carlingford. He sat down and waited at Slate Rock, where local tradition says leprechauns live in a souterrain deep under the earth's surface. Sure enough, within minutes, several leprechauns came to talk to him.

They said they were worried because of falling numbers. There are only 236 leprechauns left in Ireland, because so few people believe in them: they have been forced to emigrate. They told him that Irish leprechauns are an endangered species and need to be protected. As a result, Kevin applied to the EU, asking them to pass a law making leprechauns on Slieve Foy a protected species. They refused, stating that nobody could prove that leprechauns exist.

Kevin said, 'That was really annoying. It took me nine years to make those foolish EU bureaucrats pass a law protecting the leprechauns on Slieve Foy. Eventually they did so because I insisted they couldn't prove leprechauns don't exist.'

Slieve Foy, and in particular the area around Slate Rock, is now a protected area which is included under the EU Habitats Directive that protects the flora, fauna and leprechauns. If you don't believe me, look it up.

I asked Kevin Woods, the McCollite, why the leprechauns he talks to today are so much smaller than leprechauns in the past. He said as their numbers have decreased, so has the energy they can produce. They cannot muster enough to look as large as they once did. Also, they are spirits and materialise in different ways to different people.

According to folklore, leprechaun gold is buried in the Cooley Mountains. Every year a gold hunt is held during the Carlingford Festival. Anyone can join and people come from miles around. If you want to have a chance of finding gold on Slieve Foy, you can buy a license in O'Hare's Spirit Grocer's Shop.

I may be sceptic in thinking the local tourist board doesn't really believe in fairies; just in attracting visitors. That doesn't alter the fact that the Leprechaun Hunt is great craic and well worth joining. However, personally I am convinced some year somebody will find real leprechaun gold, not just stuff planted by the tourist board. That'll shuck them.

2

MOYRY CASTLE'S KILLER CAT

I always loved telling this story because of the audience reaction to the play on words as the killer cat compiles a catalogue of cats prepared to send humans into a state of catalepsy and so on.

The more I think about it, the more I am convinced the story contains a hidden meaning which is applicable today. The cat and his master, the wizard, were prepared to live off the environment in a sustainable fashion until a foolish human upset the balance. Thoughtlessly killing the wizard caused the cat to become filled with bloodlust with unexpected consequences. Today we are suffering from global warming with acid rain, diseased trees and so on because we are thoughtless and are not taking sufficient care of our environment.

Close your eyes in the valley leading through the Slieves of Armagh and the Mountains of Louth and you can almost hear the sound of war. The battle cry '*croachan*', the clash of swords, the groans of the wounded, the stench of death. There is a strange haunting atmosphere. This is 'The Gap of the North', where birds never sing as a mark of respect to the dead and the air seems filled with ghosts. It was the scene of many fierce battles, a 'real Bearna Baoghall', a Gap of Danger.

It was here that Hugh O'Neill fought Queen Elizabeth I's soldiers during the Nine Years' War. Eventually, after much bloodletting, the Deputy Lieutenant of Ireland, Lord Mountjoy, managed to conquer the pass after the besieged O'Neill ran out of ammunition and retreated. Mountjoy kept control of the border zone by building Moyry Castle in 1601 in the Gap of the North. Moyry Castle is an Elizabethan tower house, the stark ruined skeleton of which dominates the pass and adds to the atmosphere of desolation.

Moyry Castle was originally a simple building with different levels connected by ladders, not stairs. It was surrounded by a stout, protective bawn wall and, because of its defensive position, it had an unusual number of gun emplacements. There was a drawbridge leading to the entrance and a hole above the door used to pour boiling oil and other deterrents on to unwanted visitors. Deputy Mountjoy stationed a warden and a garrison of men in the castle to control border movement.

One day, as the sentries walked the ramparts, they saw a strange, old man with a large tiger cat coming out of the woods and heading towards them. The old man was wearing native Gaelic costume but there was something strange and foreign-looking about his lean, tanned face and the way he moved. He looked somehow as if it had come from the East. He approached the drawbridge and asked permission to enter and entertain the troops.

When questioned, he said he was a wizard who had visited all the principal castles and families in the country. The guards invited him in and enjoyed his skill in juggling and his magic tricks. Most of all they appreciated the fantastic feats performed by his tiger cat, who could jump through rings of fire. They were intrigued and asked how he had come to own such a wonderful creature. The wizard said, 'I rescued him when he was a tiny cub. He had been abandoned by his mother. I hand reared him, slept with him at night and gave him milk whenever he appeared hungry. You know something, I learnt to love that big cat as if he was my own child and it loves me. He's very affectionate and follows me around like a dog, protecting me and keeping anyone from hurting me. He can be the wild fierce boy, so he can, but the funny thing is, he likes my friends.'

Every time the cat performed a trick, the wizard petted it and gave it a little catnip treat. It rolled over in delight and purred loudly.

When they finished their performance, the guards gave the wizard gifts. He bowed and said he would call again sometime.

The two strange friends went and lived in a cave in the mountains. Each day the wizard sent the beast out to forage for food and he gave a shrill whistle when he wanted the animal to return. He replied with a loud 'murrow' and came bounding back, carrying prey in his mouth.

The big cat was an expert hunter. He didn't kill for pleasure; just sufficient to feed his master and himself. The wizard always rewarded it by stroking him, petting him and giving him little catnip treats. He cooked the prey over an open fire before dividing it into two portions and giving one to his friend. After dark the big cat and the wizard slept curled up together, covered by furs on a soft pile of leaves. They looked as snug as a pair of bugs in a rug.

Eventually the wizard decided they'd spent enough time in the one place and they should set out on their travels again. They were away for a long time and when they came back, the guards at Moyry Castle had changed. The new guards were suspicious of strangers and not nearly as friendly as the old ones. When the wizard went up to the drawbridge, the sentry lifted his bow, took aim and shot him through the heart. The cat stood still, shocked and furious at the death of his master. He took a deep breath and leapt soundlessly up on the ramparts. The sentry stiffened. He hadn't seen the cat, just a shadow and wondered what was going on.

'Who goes there?' he shouted.

'Murrow,' mewed the cat.

The sentry laughed. 'You Irish have very peculiar names. Well Murrow, where do you come from?'

'Maaa-yo.'

All cats come from Mayo.

'Give me the password,' demanded the sentry.

'Three blind mice,' replied the cat.

'Rats,' shouted the sentry.

A red cloud of rage passed before the cat's eyes at the sentry's rudeness. He crouched down, his eyes closed to narrow slits of hate. He pounced and sank his teeth into the sentry's skull, which shattered with a terrible crunching sound. The noise woke a second sentry who was dozing on the other side of the keep. He came round to see what was happening. The cat made a second spring, knocked him over and tore his throat out. His severed arteries spurted blood all over the cat's immaculate fur, turning it bright red.

The sight of so much blood caused the tiger cat to be seized by a ferocious bloodlust. He went from room to room, silently slithering down ladders and finding the garrison's soldiers sleeping in their beds. He killed them all, one by one, cracking their skulls open and shredding their flesh into mincemeat.

He then turned his rage on the countryside, killing all the animals he met, dragging their bodies back to the castle and devouring them. His shadow slid through the woods like a grim, silent ghost. He no longer killed to survive. He killed for pleasure. He became convinced all humans were evil, except his master, who he thought of as the exception that proves the rule. He watched for travellers and if they showed any sign of fear he was on them like a tornado, shattering their skulls and tearing their throats out. When he finished hunting, he sat upright on the castle ramparts and howled horribly.

Once he captured a toddler, who'd run some distance in front of its mother. The big cat picked it up in his jaws, carried it off to a clearing in the woods, set it on the ground and played cat and mouse by allowing it to crawl to the edge of the thicket before pouncing and carrying it back to the centre of the clearing in his ferocious jaws. Then he terrified the infant by hiding in a thicket, suddenly springing out and growling ferociously.

The poor child was very scared and screamed loudly. Luckily, a group of O'Hanlon's men were out hunting. They heard the screams and went to investigate. When they saw what was happening, they rushed at the cat with their long spears. The cat fought bravely before, realising it was outnumbered, backing into a thicket and snarling fiercely before disappearing into the woods with its tail swooshing in uncontrollable rage.

The toddler wasn't hurt, apart from a few minor scratches, and was taken back to his mother, who couldn't believe her eyes. She had given her son up for dead and was weeping bitterly.

Never before had the countryside been plagued by such terror. People became petrified of venturing out alone. They even went in groups to draw water from the wells. Many attempts were made to capture the killer cat but it was as clever and cunning as it was cruel. Once, when surrounded by O'Hanlon's retainers in a wood, it sprang up a tree and mocked the men by putting its nose round the trunk and laughing as arrows pinged into the bark. Eventually it sprang over their heads and vanished.

Traps and snares were set but the beast appeared to have a sixth sense warning of danger and avoided them all. The cat made its home in the castle and could be seen every night sitting proudly on the battlements. Gradually the pain caused by the loss of his master faded and he began to enjoy his solitary life. Being alone had advantages: he could come and go as he pleased. Hunting was easier because he had only one mouth to feed. The cat began to think of itself as King of the Castle. After all, he had captured and held his new home against all comers. As the cat grew more and more confident he became more and more ambitious.

He wanted to be recognised as King of the Cats, a Catamount. He came to realise he was free. No human could tell him what to do. Then he thought all cats should be free. Humans should not be allowed the keep cats as slaves; it was against their cat rights. He decided to start a cat-league for the emancipation of cats.

One night he felt the time was ripe for a revolution and stood erect on Moyry Castle's battlements. He blew a cat-call, summoning all the cats in the neighbourhood to come and hear what he had to say. He stood proudly on his hind legs with his front paws supported on a battlement and addressed the crowd.

'Friends,' he mewed loudly, ' Cats should not be held in captivity by humans. They should be free. I say by Bubastis, the wife of Pthah and the goddess of cats, at whose shrine we worship, slavery must cease. We cats must stop exterminating rats and mice because humans hate them. What harm has a rat or a mouse done to a cat? We have become nothing more than people pleasers. We must stop, unite and organise ourselves into a society with the sole aim of killing humans. Each cat must put its name in a catalogue as a Member of the League for the Extermination of the Human Race and the Emancipation of Cats. We shall no longer be catspaws. We shall become the cats' pyjamas, cause a catastrophe and wipe the human race off the face of this earth. Nobody shall escape. All humans are in the same category. Now listen carefully, I want to catechise you on how to act. Catenate yourselves in a great chain, surround the houses and catacaluptify all the inhabitants. When they are seized with catalepsy lay them out on catafalques and bury them in catacombs. Tomorrow we will meet in secret, carrying catapults. Only those with cataracts may be excused. Your leading cat, your king, your Catamount, shall stand erect to receive you. Any cat that fails to come up to scratch shall be cursed and lose its nine lives. Beware of the cataclysm engineered by me, your Catamount.'

There was great yowling and clapping of paws as the cats swore they'd never lick fur again until they'd licked their enemies. The

Catamount gave them the secret sign and they disappeared, with a flick of a cat's tail, silent shadows melting into the night.

There was one kitten who did not agree with the Catamount's plans. He loved his owners. They cuddled him, gave him cream and a warm comfortable bed. He did not want to kill them, so he told them about the plot.

When the people found they were about to be attacked, they held a council of war in Chief O'Hanlon's dun. They decided that attack was the best means of defence and that a posse should be sent out to kill the Catamount.

Chief O'Hanlon disagreed. He said a posse would be too noisy. The cat would hear it coming.

'That cat is cruel and crafty,' he said. 'Think of the way it has eluded us in the past. It would be better if one well-armed person sneaked up silently, caught it off guard and slaughtered it.'

There was an argument. Nobody wanted to face the cat alone so Chief O'Hanlon offered to go and do the job himself. If he didn't come back in a reasonable time, then an armed posse should be sent out.

The mighty chief dressed in his strongest armour, fetched his longest, sharpest sword and his stoutest shield and set off. He was careful not to make a sound. When he reached the castle, he had a stroke of luck. The killer cat had eaten a feast of lamb. It felt contented and safe, so had curled up into a ball and fallen fast asleep. Chief O'Hanlon crept up and sliced its head off. As the cat's bleeding head rolled over on the ground it made a last brave effort, opened its mouth and whispered, 'My dying wish is that you tell your kitten what you have done.'

Chief O'Hanlon agreed.

When he got back to his dun and described how the dying head had told him to tell his kitten, it raised its head. It had been listening to every word while pretending to be asleep by the fire. It had signed the Catamount's catalogue and was a fully paid-up member of 'the League for the Extermination of the Human Race and the Emancipation of Cats'. Before anyone could stop it, the kitten leapt through the air and tore out Chief O'Hanlon's throat out, causing him to bled to death. It had avenged the Catamount but in so doing it paid with its own life because the horrified onlookers killed it immediately.

The little kitten who loved its owners thought it was a great pity Moyry Castle's guard had killed the wizard. If he had been welcomed there would have been no catalogue of disasters.

3

CARLINGFORD'S FAIRY HORSE

Is this story underlining the wisdom of being truthful and caring for the environment? I got it from Kevin Woods who has a sculpture of a white horse on his property.

Cocker O'Reilly was a real pain in the neck. Locals called him 'The Cocker', because he was cocksure of everything he said. He would have argued with his own shadow. Nobody could contradict him without feeling the lash of his tongue, which was sharp enough to cut hedges.

Cocker was fond of the bottle. He drank like a fish and liked nothing better than to spend an evening propping up the bar of the local pub and arguing with all and sundry. He was seldom sober and when he was drunk, his tongue became nastier and sharper than ever. He had the gift, if you'd call it a gift, of appearing right even if he was wrong. And the annoying thing was, he was rarely wrong. He insisted he never made a mistake, but then one night he made a terrible mistake that cost him dearly.

The Cocker had been drinking and carousing in a pub in Carlingford, where he spoilt the craic with his argumentative tongue and sneering comments. He got so drunk that even those who remained sober gave way to his arguments. He was eight sheets to the wind when he staggered out into the fresh air and up the mountain path leading to the wee white, thatched cottage overlooking the glen that he called 'home'.

Cocker stumbled from one side of the path to the other as he muttered, argued and laughed to himself on his way. He looked like a mad man. When he was passing the stream that runs through Mountain Park close to his path, the sound of running water made him feel very uncomfortable. He had to do what a man has to do and carelessly staggered over to the side of the road, closed his eyes and relieved himself against a hawthorn tree. The relief was wonderful. He opened his eyes and discovered, with horror, he had relieved himself on the fairy thorn planted on the fairy mound, the home of the fairy Queen Sadhbh no less. If he had been sober, he would never have dared to do such as terrible thing.

'Lorny bless us,' he muttered.

A great fear came upon him and he tried to run away but he was so frightened thinking about the bad luck the fairies would bring that his legs shook like jelly and refused to move quickly. He stumbled and fell, picked himself up, looked all around and breathed a great sigh of relief.

'At least nobody saw me,' he muttered. 'If I wasn't spotted I'm probably safe enough, as long as I never let on.'

He continued his unsteady journey uphill, looking fearfully behind him to make sure he wasn't being followed. The coast was clear. He reached his cottage, opened the door, slammed it behind him and, convinced he really was safe, threw himself on the bed and fell into a deep, drunken slumber.

The next morning he awoke and looked round his room. What was wrong? What had happened? He shivered and the hairs on the back of his neck stood up as he remembered how he'd treated a fairy thorn with disrespect. But everything appeared normal. Nothing bad had happened.

'It's alright. I must have got away with it,' he muttered. 'The fairies must have been away from home and didn't realise I made a terrible mistake.' He breathed a sigh of relief, opened the door, looked out and saw it was a beautiful day. On the path below, a

group of neighbours were looking worried and gossiping around
the fairy tree. Filled with curiosity, he strode down the path and
joined them. One of the neighbours pointed at the base of the
tree without saying a word. The Cocker looked down and saw
that twelve brightly coloured toadstools, which had been growing
there, had withered and died.

'I wonder what happened? I think the fairies must have left this
place,' one of the neighbours said. 'There will be bad luck on this
hill before the week is out. You mark my words.'

'Nonsense,' said the Cocker, 'It's nothing to do with us. Sure, I
can smell horse piss from here. That's what killed them. That's it.
Horse piss. We've no cause to worry.'

'Do you think so?'

'I know so,' replied Cocker and they all left the place feeling
much happier. After all, Cocker was never wrong.

After a hard day's work, Crocker fell into bed and slept soundly.
Next morning he was woken, as usual, by O'Loughlin's rooster
crowing loudly as it greeted the dawn.

Cocker threw his legs out of bed onto the floor. They felt peculiar.
He looked down and was horrified to find he had hooves instead of
feet. He looked at his hands. Hooves. He then realised, with horror,
that his back was bent over. He had turned into a horse, a white
horse. The fairies had taken their terrible revenge, and he no longer
had a human form. He had been turned into a white horse and there
he was stuck in his own cottage, unable to get out of the door. He
was hungry. He tried shouting, but his voice had gone. He couldn't
talk. The only thing he could do was neigh loudly.

Several days later, the neighbours realised they hadn't seen
Cocker and came to find out if something was wrong. They
opened the cottage door and found a miserable looking, hungry
horse standing forlornly inside. They chased it up into Mountain
Park, where it can still be seen on Slieve Foy Mountain above
Carlingford. From that day to this, the locals make sure all horses
are kept well away from the fairy thorn.

There is a sequel to this sad story. The fairies asked Kevin Woods,
the McCollite, the leprechaun whisperer, to remind people of the

power fairies possess by making a model of the white horse and placing it in his garden. He has also built a structure resembling the souterrain under Slate Rock so he can take children and show them a place similar to where fairies live. The McCollite did as he was asked, but one night the model horse disappeared. CCTV cameras showed a gang of four youths taking it out of his garden and stealing his tractor from a shed. Kevin promptly reported the incident to local media, declaring that the thieves who stole the horse would be cursed for evermore. The horse was replaced the following night, although unfortunately its tail had been broken. The McCollite contacted the media again, saying the curse also applied to the stolen tractor. The following day, there was some sort of fracas in Drogheda during which a youth was shot in the foot. The garda were called and recovered the tractor.

4

IRELAND'S ATLANTIS

Tom McDevitte, alias Barney McCoo, told me this story on the day we went around the Cooley Peninsula. He said he was nearing the end of his time (he was in his late 80s) and wanted me to pass his stories on so they should not die. After all, it is the story, not the teller, who is important. We stood together at the side of Carlingford Lough as he looked up into the mountains, then down into the sea where a volcanic dyke runs into the lough. His deep voice enhanced the landscape, making a magic moment. Now, a big confession: I couldn't remember the poem until years later I bought Michael G. Crawford's excellent book, *Legendary Stories of the Carlingford Lough District*, and found 'Tom's' poem, which is reproduced below.

Upon this place the Mountain's brow
Once glowed with fiery beam
And like an arrow from the bow
Out sprang the lava spring.
The word went forth, the word of woe –
The Judgment thunders pealed,
The fiery earthquake blazed below,
Its doom was sealed.
Where art thou, proud old Cahir-Linn now?
Where are thy priests of dread?

King, people, warriors, pilgrims all –
Sunk 'neath the lava bed.
The sunbeams on thy bosom wake,
But never light thy gloom,
The tempests burst, yet never shake.

Thy depths thou mighty tomb.
Time onward has fled, long years have rolled in
Since the billows first spread o'er the 'Cahir of Linn'.
At the word of the merrow, the waters divide,
And the walls of the 'Cahir' are seen 'neath the tide,
And from the Chief Temple the sound of a bell,
Comes mournfully up as if ringing their knell.

Today, Slieve Foy towers above Carlingford resembling a friend, not a foe, but that wasn't always the case. It was once an active volcano that became very angry, with disastrous consequences.

The old city of Cahir Linn, from which Carlingford takes its name, was built around a pool of fresh water in the middle of a secluded glen between Slieve Foy and Slieve Bann. It was a beautiful place.

The city's residents were fire worshippers who purified themselves by bathing in the silver pool before going to worship Lugh and Brigid, the God and Goddess of Fire. Pilgrims came from far and near, bringing gold and other precious gifts as offerings to the gods in what was known as the 'City of the Pool' or the 'Golden City', so called because the domes of temples and palaces were coated in gold.

The principal temple was in the main square. It had two large statues at its entrance – one of Brigid, the other of Lugh. Fountains played continuously beside the temple and the sacred grove around the pool.

Sometimes the sleeping volcano cast a dull red glare that flashed on the spires and minarets of the city below, making them glow with a dazzling light. It appeared heavenly to the eyes of the worshippers in Cahir. They believed Lugh, the Sun God, was clothed in garments woven from flames. Fire spirits flew around him, fanning the flames and forming shapes. Some of the shapes were beautiful, while others became dark and horrible before lighting up like the sun and melting in the fire and being replaced by salamanders.

The people of Cahir Linn worshipped fire because they believed earth was a crust over a fiery furnace and that it was necessary to placate the sun, a fire god called Grian. He swept across the sky in his fiery chariot, allowing his heat to give life to plants and animals.

Priestesses, dressed in white robes, danced in a circle around the flames. Sacrifices were offered, the temple was filled with music and worshippers prostrated themselves on the floor to satisfy the gods as candidates for high orders in the community underwent a test. They had to dance through the crackling, oil-fed flames while priests sang sacred songs around a fire of burning logs. Anyone who faltered or failed was considered unworthy to serve either Lugh or Grian.

One of the duties of the priestesses was to keep the sacred flame burning, and the chief priestess was called Aete. She was the only daughter of Carolan, King of the Sacred City. She had been promised to the gods when she was a baby and had been brought up in the holy grove since she was an infant. She was trained in all the rites of the fire and her life was dedicated to serving the spirits of Life and Fire. She was the apple of her father's eye, until she met and fell madly in love with a great champion called Colla.

When Colla first saw Aete, he couldn't keep his eyes off her. He forgot all about the fire ceremony and the fire gods. All he could think of was Aete, Aete and Aete. That night, he climbed the walls of the forbidden grove and met her in her garden.

Aete was beautiful, young and innocent. She had never met a man before, never mind had the opportunity to talk to one. She fell in love and threw caution to the winds. The young couple arranged to meet in her sacred garden every night and it was some time before the inevitable happened and they were discovered by the high priest, who told her father. Her lover managed to escape, but Aete was arrested and thrown in prison.

Some time later, a monarch from the East visited the city and King Carolan arranged a great feast in his honour. Everyone ate and drank too much and forgot to keep a close eye on Aete. Colla disguised himself as a fire priest and sneaked inside the castle. He managed to find Aete in the dungeon, released her and they fled together towards freedom. Unfortunately they were spotted by a sentry, who sent the guards after them. They were captured and imprisoned in a cell cut out of the side of the volcano. It was a terrible place because of its proximity to the volcano, which radiated heat. The young couple suffered horribly as they lay in what was really an oven. Sweat stuck their clothes to their bodies, their throats became parched, they had little water to drink and their tongues stuck to the tops of their mouths. Very little air came through the ventilators. Sleep was impossible and they began to hallucinate. Colla made a desperate attempt to escape by grabbing the bars of the cell and attempting to bend them apart. He managed only to be badly burnt and his added agony nearly drove them frantic.

Eventually, after weeks of suffering, the young couple were sent for trial.

Colla was charged with abducting a priestess and was sentenced to death by being thrown into the volcano.

Aete was charged with breaking her sacred vows as a priestess. The judges declared the gods were very angry and that the only thing they could do was to sacrifice her to the volcano along with Colla. The following day was the Festival of Beal-Tennie, which was judged to be an auspicious time for the young couple to die. King Carlan was heartbroken, but there was nothing he could do to save his beloved only daughter, of whom he had once been so proud.

At dawn on the day of the fire festival, a procession formed and carried the young lovers up to the edge of the volcano. The king, mounted on a white horse, led the way and although his heart was breaking, he managed to look very serious and stern. He was dressed from head to toe in magnificent robes made from gold, which shone like the sun. He was followed by warriors carrying their most brilliant armour and, after them, the fire priests and priestesses walked in solemn lines. Aete and Colla were bound together on a bier carried by pallbearers in the middle of the priests and priestesses. The whole procession was accompanied by musicians playing mournful music on weird pipes and it was followed by hundreds of spectators.

They passed through the streets of Cahir Linn, along the paths of the sacred grove, around the sacred pool and up, up, up the steep slopes of the fire mountain. They formed a ring around the top and the participants peered down into the cauldron of fire below.

Aete and Colla were flung into the flames. A stream of fire shot through them and they shrieked with pain as terrible salamanders and other awful fire creatures jostled against them, pushing them hither and thither through the glowing mass of flames and lava. The crater opened and the monster fire spirit looked out. Flames shot from his eyes and his face was as black as thunder. He seized his victims and tore them limb from limb. The people cheered and the fire priests called on Lugh and Brigid to accept the sacrifices.

Slieve Tennie had always been very peaceful. Nobody had any idea it could erupt. Suddenly, the volcano emitted a scorching wind like the breath of a furnace as the ground rocked, heaved, groaned and thundered. There was a blinding flash of light. Lava shot out of the crater, boiled over the top and scalded people to death. Others rushed down the mountain side. Flames shot from the ground. The stench of sulphurous fumes hung in the air. Ash, rocks and boulders rained down on the city, destroying dwellings and killing all inside. Hundreds of people died, choked by gas or buried in boiling mud. The fire priests and priestesses perished. The temple collapsed and the city sank as an enormous mouth opened under the Irish Sea. The earth sucked in an enormous amount of water that the volcano turned into steam, forcing it back along the way it had come. A tsunami formed and rushed up the bed of the Clanryne River as far as Newry. It washed away the land and made Carlingford Lough. Today, the ancient city of Cahir Linn resides beneath the waves and is known as Ireland's Atlantis.

5

THE BIRTH OF CÚCHULAINN AND NEW GRANGE

In the past, New Grange was called Brúg na Bóinne. It is where the sun god Lugh lived in his enchanted castle and where, according to folklore, Cúchulainn was born before he moved to Dun Delgan (Dundalk) This is one of Granny Henry's stories, although she didn't mention what she would have referred to as 'naughty bits'. (They came from Cecile O'Rahilly's word-by-word translation of Táin Bó Cúalnge, a manuscript originally written about 1100.)

'Your Majesty's one irresistible smasher,' exclaimed one of the laughing group of women surrounding King Conor.

'Aye, you can say that again. He's irresistible, as I know well,' giggled another, who had had too much to drink, 'but is this one wee bride who won't follow the custom by sharing the king's bed on her wedding night?'

'Do you think I'm so hard up that I have to bed my own sister?' snarled the king.

'Sire, we know grooms are grateful to you for breaking their wives in so they can enjoy a happy marriage. It's very hard work. You don't enjoy it. You do it for the sake of the kingdom and derive no pleasure from performing your duty.'

King Conor uttered a shriek of laughter as he took his place at the top table beside his sister Dechtire and her new husband King Sualtim. He lifted a golden goblet filled with mead, gulped a mouthful, then lifted his glass and proposed a toast.

'*Slanté*,' he shouted, while holding the shining goblet aloft, 'Here's to Dechtire and Sulatin. May their cess never go sour and may all their troubles be little ones.'

He turned towards Dechtire. She looked pale and strained.

'How's about ye?' he asked fondly.

'Fine,' she responded without enthusiasm, 'I'm delighted to strengthen an important treaty enabling Ulster to remain at peace. I know that's important to you and to the kingdom.'

King Conor looked worried. He loved his sister dearly.

'I wish you looked a bit happier,' he said. 'Come on, pet, cheer up. Sualtin's a good sort. He worships the ground you walk on. He'll be good to you. He's dead on.'

Dechtire smiled wanly, glanced towards her new husband and felt sick. He was so uncouth. His beard was matted with grease and his rough, calloused hands were filthy. He grinned, exposing inflamed gums with broken teeth. He grabbed her and planted an enthusiastic kiss on her lips. She tried not to shudder as his stinking breath hit her. She avoided it by wrapping her arms around him and putting her head against the rough texture of his chest. She glanced down and saw, with annoyance, the greasy stains his hands were leaving on the shimmering folds of her silken wedding dress.

'Ugh,' she thought. 'I can't stand much more of this. How will I cope with him in bed? It doesn't bear thinking about. I've got to get a breath of fresh air or I'll die.'

She pushed firmly against her new husband's muscular chest. He held her more tightly.

'You're not trying to escape, are you darling?' he jested.

'No, of course not,' she responded, 'I've got a call from nature. I'd better go outside before I act in a childish fashion.'

'Too much excitement,' laughed one of the women, 'has a bad effect on the bladder.'

'You could say that.'

Sualtin let her go. She walked gracefully out the door and fled out through the high circular earthen ditches with their sturdy wooden fences, which surrounded the fort and into the welcoming gloom of the forest. She breathed a sigh of relief.

'I wish I didn't have to face the horror of a wedding night,' she thought. 'I wish I could stay here in the clean fresh air. I wish I had a little romance in my life. I wish I was a serving girl who could marry whoever who she liked.

'Oh dear, it would be a help if I even liked Sualtin, but I can't stand him.'

A black cloud of despondency hung over her soul. She gave herself a mental shake, attempted to cheer up and whispered. 'Come on, Dechtire. Sualtin's not all bad. He's good-natured and very generous. Conor's right. He'll be kind to you. You're too fussy. He can't help having horrible black hairs sticking out of his nose and red rough horny hands. Ugh,' she shuddered at the idea of what those hands might do on their wedding night. Then she squared her shoulders and began to walk firmly back to her wedding feast.

'I might as well get on with it. There's no escape,' she muttered aloud, as she walked towards the edge of forest.

The sun shone brightly, lighting the leaves and casting shadows on the bright ground.

'Why can't you escape?' asked a melodious manly voice.

Startled, she looked around the clearing.

'Dechtire. Over here, come on. Over here,' a voice called softly from some bushes at the edge of the forest. She thought she was imagining things and continued walking slowly back to the fort.

'Darling, listen to me,' whispered the voice. 'Look behind you.'

Dechtire turned and saw a tall, handsome stranger with a long, golden beard and heavy gold torques around his neck and arms.

She looked at his merry smile and sparkling blue eyes. He was a genuine hunk.

'Who are you?' she gasped.

'Lugh.' came the quick reply.

'Lugh, the Ss-sssssuuuun God?' she stuttered.

'No less,' smiled the stranger. 'And I love you. Will you marry me and come to live with me in my enchanted castle, Brúg na Bóinne?'

'I can't do that,' whispered Dechtire. 'I don't know you.'

She shivered with desire as Lugh took her in his arms. They felt so nice, so different from the rough hug of her husband. If only. If only …'

'If only what?' asked Lugh.

'What? Have you read my thoughts?'

'Yes. We could be so close, so happy. Come, run away with me.'

'I can't do that.'

'Why not?'

'My brother's delighted I've agreed to marry Sualtin. He wants Ulster to prosper in peace. If I run away with you, there'll be a war. Hundreds of people will die and I'd be responsible for their deaths. I can't do that. It would be wrong.'

'What happens if you just disappear?'

'That'd be different. It wouldn't look as if it was my fault.'

'That's right, darling. And what if I promised to protect Conor's kingdom?'

'Can you?'

'Of course I can. I'm Lugh, the Sun God. I can do anything I choose.'

Lugh took her in his arms and kissed her gently. She felt as if she was melting into his arms.

'Great are the powers of the Otherworld. I can foresee the future. There will be important places named after me, such as London, Leicester and County Louth. Come with me and enjoy things unseen by the eyes of mere humans. Tell you what. Go back to the feast. Flirt shamelessly with Sualtin. Convince him you can't wait to get into bed with him. After a decent interval, when you feel ready, hold your glass up. I'll come in the form of a mayfly and fall into your wine. Drink it and swallow me. You'll fall into a deep sleep. Sualtin is bound to send you to rest with your girlfriends. I'll turn you, and your friends, into birds and you can fly out of the window to my enchanted castle. There we'll live happy ever after. How's that for a plan?'

Dechtire smiled, held her face up for a kiss, ran back to the feast and took her place beside her husband. He beamed with pride. He was chewing with his mouth open. It was a revolting sight.

'Sweetheart,' he muttered drunkenly, placing his hand upon her breast. 'I can't wait to get you into bed. Come on. Let's stop wasting time.'

'I can't bear this,' she thought, 'But I've got to find the strength to put on the act of a lifetime.'

She laughed merrily and raised her wine goblet.

'Husband,' she cried, 'I don't think you should drink any more. Remember, the king's my brother. He can't comfort me if your sword is rotted by booze on our wedding night. And I've some catching up to do. I must have more wine if I'm to find the courage to face your manhood.'

Dechtire held her wine glass up.

'A toast,' she cried, 'Here's to Sualtin and all men like him.'

The guests stood up.

'To Sualtin.'

As Sualtin stood up to reply, a mayfly appeared and dived into Dechtire's glass. She lifted it to her mouth, swallowed the contents in one gulp, gave a gasp, turned white and fainted.

Sualtim picked her up, carried her into her room, laid her down on her bed and asked fifty of her friends, the most beautiful girls in court, to watch over her. He tiptoed out of the room and re-joined Conor at the wedding feast.

Suddenly there was a swooshing noise, a swish and a swoosh. It startled the courtiers, who ran to the doors and windows to look. They saw a flock of white birds circling the castle, before swooping towards the south. Sualtin's heart contracted in his chest.

'Dechtire, Dechtire,' he cried. 'You haven't been stolen by the fairies, have you? Oh no. They steal beautiful brides, and you're the most beautiful bride that ever existed.'

He rushed towards her room. It was empty. He sank to his knees, put his head against the bed and sobbed his heart out.

Sualtin, King Conor and the Men of Ulster searched the countryside, endlessly looking for Dechtire. There was no sign of her.

A year later, when they were celebrating the festive season, sitting in a circle, joking and drinking mead, King Conor was in fine fettle. He rose to his feet and proposed a toast. 'Men,' he yelled, 'may you be saved from marrying wenches who blow wind like a stones from a sling.'

He glanced out the window. 'What the … ?' he shouted.

A huge black cloud hung in the sky. The sun appeared to go out as it was hidden behind a huge, cloud-like flock of birds, which covered it. At first the men were amused, then they became angry, because the birds behaved like a swarm of locusts. They laid waste to the countryside around Emain Macha. Leaves disappeared from the plants until there wasn't a single blade of grass left anywhere and the landscape appeared barren.

The Men of Ulster were furious. They hitched their horses to their chariots and set off across the country, chasing the birds south. The birds led them across County Armagh (Slieve Fuad), by Ath Lethan, by Mac Gossa, between Fir Rois and Fir Ardae (Ardee).

Dusk fell and Conor began to look for somewhere to spend the night. He spotted lights shining through the gloom. The Men of Ulster walked towards them and discovered a beautiful castle. They went up to the door, which opened immediately, and they were amazed when guards greeted each one of them by name and invited them in.

That was a great night, that was. The craic was mighty. The Men of Ulster enjoyed the food, the wine, music, dancing and the company of beautiful women.

Their hostess appeared strangely familiar. Conor kept staring at her. It couldn't be, could it? Then he realised it really was Dechtire, but Dechtire as he'd never seen her before. He got up, went over to her, smiled, held out his hand and asked for a dance.

'Are you really my little sister?' he asked as they twirled about the floor.

'None other,' she replied.

'Please Dechtire, come home with us,' he pleaded. 'We miss you terribly.'

'Can't you see I'm really happy? I love being here.'

'Please Dechtire, please come home.'

'This could be dangerous,' she thought. 'Conor's as stubborn as a mule. He'll never give up on the idea of wanting me to go back with him. He could annoy the Shee. That could be life-threatening. I can't let that happen.'

She looked up into her brother's eyes.

'Poor Conor,' she thought, as she placed a couple of her soft fingers against his lips.

'Hush,' she whispered, 'keep your counsel. Anything else could be dangerous. I'll think about it.'

Conor smiled, 'You do that, dear. Think about it and remember how much we love you.' Dechtire planted a quick kiss on his cheek, before returning to her husband.

That night, King Conor fell into a deep, contented sleep, believing his dear sister would find a way to return with him. He thought she must have wanted to see him. She must have sent the birds to lure the Men of Ulster south. Their hosts acted as if they had been expected. He was warm and comfortable as he fell asleep and it was a great shock when he awoke in a clearing in the forest. The rain was coming down in stair-rods and he was soaked. He stood up, amazed. What had happened? Where was his warm, comfortable bed? Where was Dechtire?

The men woke one by one. There were questions on every lip. Where had the castle gone? Why had it disappeared? Why were they in the middle of a forest clearing in a howling gale with the rain pelting down?

'Shush,' whispered King Conor. 'We must be patient. Did you recognise Dechtire last night? I think she intends to join us. We must be patient and wait for her.'

Dusk fell and Dechtire did not appear. Suddenly they heard a baby crying and searched their surroundings. They finally found the wee mite in a basket hidden among the willows. Conor lifted the baby up and cuddled it. He was delighted.

'This baby is a dead ringer for Dechtire,' he said, 'She must intend coming home with us. I think we should stick around a while longer.'

They waited until it was dark but Dechtire didn't come. Eventually, the Men of Ulster decided the best thing they could do was return to Emain Mach, bringing the baby with them.

Sualtim was delighted when he saw the baby.

'This child,' he declared, 'could have been my son. Look at the wee dote. He's the spitting image of Dechtire. I'll bet she's sorry she can't come to live with me. She loves me and knows I'm very lonely without her so she's sent her wee baby to keep me company. I'm going to call him Setanta, son of Sualtin. He's dead on. He'll grow up to be a great warrior, so he will, I feel that in my bones.'

6

THE HOUND
OF ULSTER

'I don't believe it,' King Conor gasped in amazement, 'surely that can't be true. It's impossible. My eyes must be deceiving me.'

'No, sire. No, they're not. Yon wee nipper really is playing hurling against the whole of the Boys' Brigade. He's a fiendish player and often challenges the rest of the brigade to a match. He can knock the stuffing out of them too.'

King Conor laughed heartily as he yelled, 'Setanta! Setanta! I'm going to visit Culan. I think it's time you had new weapons. How'd you like to come along with me and we can get you fixed up?'

Thank you Uncle King Conor. I'm winning and I'd like to finish this game. Would you mind if I did that and caught up with you later?'

'Right you are, then. See you later,' shouted King Conor as he started out on his journey.

Culan was an expert blacksmith. He loved his job, the sense of power as he used the bellows to make the fire red hot. When the metal melted he enjoyed the steady thud, thud of the hammer on the anvil and the feel of his powerful muscles in action. He took great pride in his work and could fashion the finest needles.

'It's dead easy to make a crude chunky thing like a horse shoe, or a poker,' he said, 'but needles. That's a different ball game entirely. It's really difficult. The metal has to be drawn out into a very thin line. It has to have a sharp point to puncture cloth and an eye through which it can be threaded. I can make the finest needles with the sharpest point. Needles have magic powers. If you point a needle at a stye in the eye, it will be cured.'

Culan was in great demand. King Conor himself was a patron and Culan became very wealthy. But, like many wealthy men, he was a terrible worrier. He worried in case he lost King Conor's custom or in case he was attacked by thieves and had his wealth stolen.

Culan's worry about being burgled persisted, so he built a strong palisade round his property, then thought fences can be breached. He hired guards, but guards could be bribed. He woke one night with a brilliant idea. What he needed was a guard dog, a ferocious hound that was trained to kill on sight. A dog could not be bribed and had the added advantage of not needing to be paid. He searched the length and breadth of Ireland and eventually found an ugly, bad-tempered beast. It looked like a devil. It was pure white with red eyes that glowed in the dark and it growled incessantly. Culan loved it and, strangely enough, it loved Culan, who kept it chained up during the day and released it at dusk. The hound was a great success. It attacked intruders on sight. One night, though, it howled horribly and disturbed Culan's sleep.

'I should go see what's wrong,' he thought sleepily, but he was snug and comfortable. It was raining outside and blowing a gale, so he cuddled up against his wife's warm body and went back to sleep. The next day he went to chain his guard dog up and found it covered in blood and chewing a tough leather boot. He looked around and found another boot inside the compound. There was no other sign of an intruder. When Culan examined the boots, he discovered they had feet inside them. His hound must have devoured the intruder. Culan was delighted.

'Aren't you the quare snick,' he said, petting the animal. 'Who's a clever boy then? Did a bad, bad man disturb you last night?

Did that bad, bad man come to steal my money? And what did you do? You ate him all up and made him all done, so you did. Thon was a great deed. It's a pity those boots are so tough and you couldn't get his feet and eat them too. Still, people will believe you eat intruders when they see those feet in boots. That'll harden their groins. They mightn't believe me otherwise. You're a great dog.'

Culan showed all his friends and acquaintances the feet in the boots. As a result, the fame of his hound spread throughout the land and no robber even thought about breaking into his property.

When King Conor arrived at Culan's dun, he was made very welcome. He settled down by the fire with a beer in one hand and his eyes on the dancing girls. One of them had an especially delicious wiggle and a figure to die for. He sat goggling, his eyes out on stalks, and completely forgot about Setanta.

'Is everyone inside?' asked Culan. 'I'm going to let the hound out.'

It grew dark. All was peaceful until the silence was shattered by a terrible noise. The hound began barking and howling, while a voice guldered the ancient war cry. '*Croachan*! *Croachan*! *Croachan*!'

'By all ye gods,' gasped King Conor, 'I forgot all about Setanta. He said he'd join me once he'd finished his hurling match.'

Culan went white, immediately thinking that if his hound ate Setanta he'd be bound to lose the king's patronage. He opened the door and peered out into the gloom. One of the women screamed, 'It's a ghost!'

A large white shape was raising itself up into the air and banging its head against the ground. The air was filled with shouts and a terrible choking rasping sound.

'Oh deary me! Oh dear me,' sobbed one of the women. 'Poor wee Setanta. He was such a bright, plucky, wee thing. He's killed Culan's hound by sticking in its throat. Oh deary me, oh deary me.'

Flaming torches were hastily fetched to light the compound. Culan groaned while King Conor breathed a sigh of relief. Setanta had the hound by the feet and was banging its head against the ground.'

Culan completely forgot the king's presence and yelled with rage, 'What in the name of all that's wonderful are you doing to my dog?'

'Putting it out of its misery.'

'What do you mean "putting it out of its misery"?'

'I mean, when I arrived I couldn't get in. The gate was locked so I did my salmon leap and jumped over the fence. I was walking towards the door when this hound ran towards me. It was growling like mad and its eyes were awful. Red they were, full of hate. I remembered it ate a man, all apart from his feet, which were protected by his boots. It intended eating me, so it did. I didn't want to kill the brute, so I didn't. I thought I'd knock it out with my hurling ball, you know the one you gave me, Uncle King Conor, with the silver bands round it. I put the ball on the ground, lifted my hurling stick and aimed it at the dog's forehead. I thought I'd knock it out but it opened its mouth and the ball went down its throat. The poor thing was in agony so I decided the best thing I could do was put it out of its misery. That's why I bashed its brains against the ground.'

Culan was so upset he forgot all about the king's patronage and guldered, 'That's all very well for you, you varmint, you! You've killed my guard dog! How do I protect my compound now?'

Setanta said, 'That's easy. Your hound sired some fine pups, didn't it? Train one of the pups. I'll guard your compound 'until it's ready to take over the job.'

Cúchulainn looked at King Conor and asked, 'What do you think of that?'

King Conor smiled. 'I reckon Setanta's better at guarding compounds than any dog. After all, he managed to kill your hound, didn't he?'

So it was agreed. Setanta took the place of Culan's hound and was nicknamed Cú Culan, 'cú' meaning 'hound'. Therefore,

Cúchulainn means Culan's hound. The story of Culan's hound spread through the whole of Ireland.

Queen Maeve of Roscommon was very ambitious. She wanted to expand her territory and laughed and laughed and laughed at the story.

'This is my opportunity,' she said. 'Ulster's reduced to promot-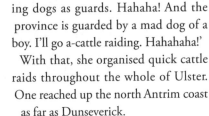ing dogs as guards. Hahaha! And the province is guarded by a mad dog of a boy. I'll go a-cattle raiding. Hahahaha!'

With that, she organised quick cattle raids throughout the whole of Ulster. One reached up the north Antrim coast as far as Dunseverick.

7

CÚCHULAINN BECOMES A WARRIOR AND SEEKS ADVENTURE

Cúchulainn was fed up. Everybody was busy doing something while he was moseying around, bored, filling time. Idly he picked up his hurling stick with the special ball King Conor had given him and hit it an almighty clout. He ran after it and held his breath as it hit the wall of Cathbad's house. Cathbad did not take kindly to boys who disturbed his peace by banging their balls against his walls. He stood motionless, waiting for Cathbad's familiar angry roar. All was silent. He crouched low to avoid being spotted and crept noiselessly towards his ball. As he picked it up he stopped, rooted to the spot. One of Cathbad's students was asking a very interesting question. 'Please Lord Wizard, will you tell us if the signs say it is a good or a bad day to start a new project?'

'That's easy,' Cathbad smiled, 'the signs say if a warrior takes arms today he will become the greatest champion Ireland has ever known, but, he will not live to be old.'

Cúchulainn felt the hairs on the back of his neck rise up with excitement. 'Hell's bells and buckets of blood,' he gasped, 'I've wanted to be a great warrior since I was a wee nipper … I don't care if I die young. Better a short life remembered than a long one forgotten.' He picked up his ball and stick and ran into King Conor's bedchamber.

King Conor awoke with a start. He was not pleased. He had a hangover.

'In the name of all that's wonderful what on earth do you mean, blattering in here and disturbing my sleep? Have you no respect?' Conor was tired. He'd had a rough night and sat up in bed feeling grumpy. His head ached and his mouth felt as if it was full of old socks.

'Why are you wakening me up at this ungodly hour?' he grunted. 'You deserve a good kicking.'

'Please Uncle King, please excuse me, but it's vital that I take up arms today.'

'You're far too young,' Conor moaned. 'You must be half a sandwich short of a picnic to have a crazy notion like that in your head. Who gave you that looney idea anyway?'

'Cathbad the Druid,' Cúchulainn replied.

'Are ye sure?'

'Aye, I'm sure. Cathbad said so.'

'Alright then. I'm coming. I suppose I'll have to. Who am I to argue with Cathbad? He might put a spell on me and make all my teeth fall out,' Conor groaned as he crawled out of bed.

'Come on, ye young rascal, ye. Follow me. We'd better go to the armoury to see if we can find suitable weapons.'

When they reached the armoury, he gave Cúchulainn a shield and two spears. Cúchulainn smashed them to smithereens. Conor lifted another shield and two more spears. Cúchulainn smashed them too. Conor gave Cúchulainn more and still more weapons and Cúchulainn smashed the lot, causing Conor to look at him in amazement. It was hard to believe someone so young could be so strong. Eventually Conor sighed and grumbled, 'I give up. You can have my weapons.'

Cúchulainn took King Conor's weapons and did his best to smash them. They stayed intact, and he smiled with satisfaction as Cathbad came into the armoury.

'Cúchulainn, what on earth are you up to?' he asked.

'Cathbad, do you mean to say you didn't tell Cúchulainn to take up arms today?'

Cathbad looked thoughtful. 'I wouldn't want his mother's son to take arms to day.'

'You lied!' King Conor yelled, shaking his fist at Cúchulainn. 'You disturbed my sleep for nothing and caused untold damage to weapons and chariots. What are you up to, you ramscallion, you?'

'Please believe me. I didn't lie. I overheard Cathbad say any warrior taking arms for the first time today would be the greatest warrior in Ireland but he'd have a short life.'

'That's true,' said Cathbad, 'Take arms today and have a great name, great fame and die young. I wouldn't wish your mother's son to do that.'

'I don't care if I should only live one day and one night, as long as my name and my story live after me. I want to be remembered.'

King Conor looked very upset. He was delighted at Cúchulainn's ambition, but he loved his nephew and hated the idea of him dying young.

'Come on, ye wee devil's imp,' he said, 'Let's see if we can find a chariot for you.'

Cúchulainn climbed into the first chariot Conor produced, jumped up and down, made it sway and shake and smashed it to smithereens. He climbed into a second chariot and broke it too. Then, one by one, he broke all the chariots Conor had put aside for the use of the Boys' Brigade and all the young warriors.

'Alright, alright,' the king groaned, 'You've wakened me out of my sleep, you've wheedled me out of my arms so you might as well have my chariot too. And I suppose I must lend you Ibar, my own special chariot driver. That way you have the lot and I've nothing left apart from a sore head and a lack of sleep.'

Conor went to Ibar, his charioteer, and said to him quietly, 'I'm worried about Cúchulainn. He's determined to take arms today. Do your best to keep the wee lad out of trouble. You know what he's like.'

Ibar smiled. 'That's fine. I'm fond of the lad but I can't promise to keep him out of trouble. You know what he's like.' Ibar drove King Conor's chariot over to Cúchulainn, who jumped in, took the horses' reins and began to jump up and down and to sway from side to side. He was unable to smash it.

'This chariot's dead on, Uncle King Conor,' he shouted. 'Thanks a bucket.'

Cúchulainn got the feel of his weapons by asking Ibar to drive the chariot three times round Emain Macha. When he saw the Boy's Brigade exercising, he drew himself to his full height and asked Ibar to drive him past the boys. He had a terrible urge to show off.

'Yhippee,' they shouted. 'Look at our Cú. He'll be the quare pup when he grows a tail.'

Cúchulainn then asked Ibar to drive him to the Ulster border.

'Are you mad, Cú?' asked Ibar. 'Thon countryside's dangerous, to put it mildly.'

'Come on Ibar,' Cúchulainn ordered, 'Get your finger out. Stop being such a big girl's blouse. We're going to cross the border and that's that.'

Ibar shook his head while taking comfort from the fact that the border guards were very alert. They'd recognise King Conor's chariot and wouldn't let it pass. With any luck he'd end up having a good day out with Cúchulainn. He took the horses' reins and sat back contentedly, enjoying the rumble of the chariot wheels against the ground, the smell of the horses, the sound of their hooves, the clear air and the sun shining through the leaves of the ancient oak forest surrounding the Gap of the North.

Conall was guarding the border. He glared at Cúchulainn.

'Clear off,' he shouted, 'you should be back in the nursery, not out here. It's too dangerous for kids.'

'I'll guard the border,' Cúchulainn replied in a grand manner. 'I've taken arms. I'm a fully fledged warrior.'

'Feel yer head,' snarled Conall, 'You haven't even got a beard. Clear off, you young whippersnapper, you. Away and scratch yourself.'

Cúchulainn ignored Conall and asked Ibar to drive on. Conall was worried. He'd be in serious trouble if anything happened to Cúchulainn. He was the king's nephew, after all. He turned his chariot and raced after him.

Cúchulainn glanced behind.

'Drat,' he muttered. 'When I do a great deed Conall will claim credit for it. I must get rid of him.' He bent down, picked up a rock, took aim and threw it at Conall's chariot. He hit the yoke. It broke. Conall tumbled out of his chariot, landed on the ground with a heavy thud and hurt his shoulder.

'May the hens of hell roast on your chest,' he shouted, 'I hope you're attacked and killed. Shove it up you sideways.'

Ibar couldn't help laughing as he said, 'How about a visit to the seaside?'

Cúchulainn smiled as he said, 'Yon would be wheeker.'

They went to Carlingford Lough (Fertais Locha Echtrand) and enjoyed spending a quiet time rock climbing and fishing. Eventually Ibar turned to Cúchulainn and said, 'We'd better go home now. Doesn't time fly when you're happy?'

Cúchulainn was worried. He'd enjoyed himself but hadn't had a big adventure and the day was coming to an end. He'd better do something drastic. 'What are those mountains?' he asked.

'The Mountains of Mourne,' Ibar replied.

'Well,' said Cúchulainn, pointing upwards to the top of a mountain, 'I want to go to that cairn up there.'

'Come on then,' sighed Ibar, 'you're the boss.' He turned the chariot and followed the road from County Louth into County Down.

Cúchulainn was intrigued by the view from the cairn and asked Ibar to point out all the landmarks. Ibar pointed across the border towards the fort belonging to Nechta's sons, who boasted that they had killed more Ulster men than were left living.

'That's it,' Cúchulainn said, 'I'll kill Nechta's three sons.'

Ibar tried to argue with him. 'For goodness sake, don't go back over the border, Cú,' he said, 'I'm starving with hunger and I've such a thirst on me I could lick moisture off a cow's bum through a bush.'

'Forget your stomach.' Cúchulainn demanded. 'There's a job to do. Nechta's sons have killed a wheen of Ulster men. I must challenge them. You're not my nursemaid. King Conor told you to do as I say. Now drive me back into County Louth to Nechta's fort.'

Ibar was very anxious as he turned the chariot towards the border.

Nechta's fort had a large pool in front of it as well as a green with a large standing stone. Cúchulainn climbed out of the chariot, went over to the stone, read the Ogham writing attached to it by a peg and shouted, 'This stone says it's *tabu* for any warrior to walk on this green without challenging for single combat.'

'Come on Cú, never mind what it says. Let's go home.' Ibar pleaded.

Cúchulainn shook his head, 'Hundreds of brave Ulster men have died here. I've gotta revenge them.' He wrapped his arms around the standing stone, heaved it out of position, staggered over to the pool and threw it in. It sank in the murky depths without leaving a trace.

'Cúchulainn! You're not the full shilling,' gasped Ibar. 'Let's get out of here.'

'No,' snapped Cúchulainn. 'You're nothing but a cissy talking like that. 'I'm not going home 'til I've killed Nechta's sons. I'll have a wee snooze in the back of the chariot until somebody worth fighting turns up.'

Ibar arranged rugs and furs for Cúchulainn, who lay down and fell fast asleep. Ibar breathed a sigh of relief.

'Now the wee nipper's out of sight,' he thought, 'he can't get into trouble. With any luck, Nechta will see a charioteer resting his horses and not bother with me. We'll be fine as long as Cú doesn't waken up.'

Suddenly, Nechta's eldest son appeared. 'Driver,' he snapped, 'unharness those horses and yer're dead.'

'Wouldn't dream of it,' trembled Ibar, 'the reins are still in my hands. I've come a long way and just need a little rest.'

The eldest son looked more closely. 'Those horses belong to King Conor,' he commented. 'Who's inside the chariot?'

'Only a young lad. He's fooling around, playing at taking arms. You know what young fellas are like. We're going. Sorry to have troubled you.' He drove the chariot forward. Cúchulainn woke up.

'What's happening?' he shouted, wiping the sleep out of his eyes, 'Where are we going?' He caught sight of the eldest son and was immediately wide awake. He grabbed his sword and shield, jumped out of the chariot and yelled, 'I challenge you to single combat!'

The eldest son nearly laughed his leg off. He towered over Cúchulainn and looked down his nose.

'I don't fight mere pups,' he sneered.

Cúchulainn kicked his shin. The eldest son flew into a rage.

'Come on! You're yellow! You're chicken, so ye are!' yelled Cúchulainn as he kicked the other shin. 'Come and fight. Scaredy, scaredy custard! Scaredy, scaredy custard!'

Nechta's eldest blew his top. 'You varmint, you!' he shouted as he drew his sword, 'I'll teach you a lesson you won't forget!'

He swiped at Cúchulainn, who ducked and dodged his feet spinning in an intricate pattern on the damp grass. At last Cúchulainn saw his chance, lifted a stone and flung it with all his might. It hit the warrior's forehead, making his skull ring like a bell. The stone flew out the other side of his head, his brains splattered on the ground and it was possible to see daylight through the hole. As the warrior fell, Cúchulainn swung his sword with a great upward swipe, cutting through the dead man's neck with such force that the head flew up in the air. Cúchulainn caught it as it fell towards earth and, with a cry of triumph, hung it by the hair on his chariot. The lips of the head grimaced in death, then all was still.

Ibar cheered, 'Good on ye, Cú! You're some pup!'

The second son came rushing out, saw his brother's severed head, yelled, '*Croachan!*' raised his sword and rushed towards Cúchulainn.

Cúchulainn took careful aim and threw his spear with all his strength. The spear soared through the air, passed through the warrior's chest and embedded itself in the soft turf. Cúchulainn cut the head off and hung it on the chariot. 'Two down, one to go,' he said.

There was a shriek of rage as the third son appeared. He fancied himself as a champion swimmer.

'Come on,' he bellowed as he leapt into the pool. 'Let's see how you get on in water.'

Cúchulainn immediately jumped into the pool, which was so deep that the warriors could not touch the bottom. He watched his chance to lunge forward and stick his sword through the third son's heart. When Cúchulainn cut the head off, the rest of the body drifted away, spouting blood as it disappeared from sight. The once black water turned red while Cúchulainn and Ibar stood admiring the brother's heads hanging on the chariot.

'GEE! You're some pup!' said Ibar in an admiring fashion. 'I've never seen the like.

Cúchulainn blushed with pleasure.

'You're not too bad yourself,' he said. 'Come on. We're wasting time. Let's pillage the fort and set it on fire.'

'I love a good pillage,' smiled Ibar.

They ravaged the fort then watched it burn.

'That's that,' said Cúchulainn. 'We have revenged all the Men of Ulster who were killed by those evil brothers.'

'Time for home,' said Ibar. 'You've done a great deed so now we can think of our bellies. My stomach thinks my throat's cut.'

Ibar turned the chariot and they sped towards Emain Macha. Cúchulainn was delighted with himself. He sat bolt upright, his sword in one hand, his shield in the other and scanned the countryside for another adventure. He spotted a herd of deer. 'Ibar,' he shouted, 'catch up with that herd.'

Ibar urged the horses forward. They galloped as fast as they could but the deer outpaced them.

'King Conor's horses are fat freaks,' grumbled Cúchulainn, 'they couldn't catch their granny in a field.'

He threw down his arms, grabbed a couple of ropes, leapt out of the chariot and sped after the deer. He lassoed a stag with one hand while his other hand threw another rope into the air. It snaked forward and landed, as if by magic, around the neck of another stag.

'Yhippeeeeeeee!' yelled Cúchulainn, digging his heels into the earth so that sparks flew from them. 'Yhippeeeeee!'

The stags pulled and pulled but were helpless in Cúchulainn's grasp. They became dispirited and walked quietly, like dogs, allowing themselves to be led to the chariot and tied on the back.

'It's dead easy to kill game,' he said. 'It takes hunting skill to capture it alive.'

Ibar gasped with astonishment as Cúchulainn nonchalantly climbed back into the chariot. He looked up, saw a flock of swans flying overhead, lifted a small stone, took aim and threw it into the air. Eight swans fell to the ground, stunned.

Cúchulainn snorted in disgust. 'That's a dead loss. I can do better.' He lifted a large stone and threw it at the swans. Sixteen fell to the ground. He lifted them into the chariot and tied them up in case they recovered and escaped.

Cúchulainn was as proud as punch and stood up straight in the chariot as they approached Emain Macha.

A small boy was playing outside. He looked up and saw the chariot in the distance. He was curious, so climbed up on top of the ramparts so he could see better. Some friends joined him and strained their eyes into the dusk. Several adults wondered what the boys were looking at and climbed up beside them.

'Ye gods and little fishes, what's that?' they asked. 'It's going at a quare lick or it wouldn't be kicking up so much dust.'

'Am I a raving looney or do I see King Conor's horses?'

'They can't be the king's horses. I saw him a short time ago.'

'Aye. He's around all right. But, as far as I know, he lent his chariot to Cúchulainn.'

'He WHAT?'

'Do you think yon's Cú's in thon chariot?'

'I do.'

'Lorney bless us. Yon could be dangerous.'

'You're dead right. When yon wee lad's in one of his odd moods, you'd never know what he'd get up to.'

'Look! Thon's Cú alright, and look at the cut of him.'

'Aye, I can't say I like the look of thon.'

'I don't believe it. He's got a load of deer tied on to back of the chariot and they're running along like tethered horses.'

'OHHHHHHHHHHHHHH! He's got human heads tied by their hair on the front of the chariot!'

'He's in one of his moods.'

'He'll murder us!'

'Quick! Quick! Fetch King Conor. He'll know what to do.'

The crowd roared, 'Fetch King Conor! Fetch King Conor!'

King Conor looked and exclaimed, 'Hell's bells and buckets of blood! We must calm him down. Quick! Get three vats of cold water. We'll throw him in one after another. That should cool his ardour.'

'If we can get him in.'

'You're right,' agreed King Conor. 'Now let's think … Oh, I think I've got it! Cúchulainn's a shy sort of lad. Find as many young good-looking girls as possible. Get them here pronto. This is an emergency.'

Nine young girls ran towards the king.

'Girls,' ordered Conor, 'get your kit off. Cú's in one of his moods and we've got to calm him down. He's easily embarrassed. If he's sees a bunch of stark staring naked women cheering, it's bound to scare the life out of him. He'll not know what to do, or where to look. We'll be able to grab him and cool him down by shoving him in cold water.'

The girls quickly stripped naked and were joined by others, so Cúchulainn was cheered by 100 naked women at the entrance of Emain Macha. He turned crimson and kept his eyes firmly fixed on his feet. Ibar couldn't keep from chuckling.

'King Conor's a wily auld divil,' he muttered to himself as he drew the chariot up beside the three vats of cold water.

King Conor nearly died laughing at the expression on Cúchulainn's face.

Eager hands lifted Cúchulainn out of the chariot and ducked him in the first vat. His over-excited body caused the vat to burst open. Water cascaded around the men holding Cúchulainn and made them fall over each other. They scrambled up, grabbed Cúchulainn and threw him into the second vat. The water seethed, making waves travel over its surface. Finally, the men managed to lift Cúchulainn out and immerse him in the third vat. They held onto him as the water became very hot.

Cúchulainn looked up quietly and smiled. 'I'm a real warrior at last,' he said.

8

THE PILLOW FIGHT
AND CATTLE RAID

I loved granny telling me this story; it was so much fun. We giggled over the ridiculous fight between Queen Maeve and her husband. Granny explained how a silly argument caused Queen Maeve to invade County Louth where the weight of her army was so great its passage compacted the Cooley Mountains, forming the Windy Gap.

Years later, I discovered the king and queen were arguing after they had made love and that made the whole situation seem even more ridiculous. At the time, all granny said was, 'Imagine fighting over your possessions. They can make you very unhappy, if you let them. Sometimes, the more you have, the more you want. Queen Maeve and King Ailill should have been concentrating on the love they had for each other, not on the things they had.'

I loved the way granny sat up straight and flung her arms out when describing the battle: 'And Cúchulainn cut off 200 hundred heads with one almighty swipe of his sword.'

'Granny,' I always protested, 'nobody could do that. It's impossible.'

'Child, dear. He was the Champion of Champions and a great hero to boot. He could do extraordinary deeds. And you never know what you can do until you try.'

Queen Maeve lay back, daydreaming on her pillows.

King Ailill climbed out of bed, grunted and attempted to attract her attention by parading naked around the room. He caught a glimpse of himself in the mirror. There was no doubt about it, he was a fine figure of a man.

Maeve continued to daydream.

Ailill felt annoyed. He knew he was attractive. He had just made passionate love to his wife. She had enjoyed it, but she was not looking grateful. She was ignoring him. It was not right. She was an ungrateful hussy. Maeve stretched out, her long naked body gleaming like silk in the candlelight.

Ailill glowered at her. She was beautiful, but ungrateful. He realised she was deep in thought because her eyes had turned red and the pupils were moving from side to side.

'How dare she look like that after I've made love to her?' he thought. 'She's thinking about something and it's not about ME.'

Maeve appeared completely unaware of him. He went outside and stood for several minutes gazing at the stars. It was a bright clear night. The moon had a red ring around it.

'A storm's brewing,' he thought. He leaned against the doorpost, watched his wife for several minutes then glanced down at his fine muscular body. Maeve still appeared unaware of his presence.

'Maeve,' he complained loudly, 'you are very lucky to have a fine husband, like me. The very least, you could do is give me a little attention.'

'What's that you said?' Maeve asked, suddenly focusing her eyes on him.

He recognised the danger signs. She was scowling and her eyes were burning like two coals in her head. 'I said, you are very lucky to have me as a husband.'

'Why?'

'It's obvious,' replied Ailill. 'You were lucky to be able to marry a king.'

'Feel your head, you nincompoop, you!' snapped Maeve, 'I am, and was, a queen. I could have married a swineherd and remained a queen. Your title means nothing to me.'

'Your head's cut,' growled Ailill. 'You were lucky to catch me. You can't say I'm not great in bed and I'm very rich.'

'Twaddle,' snarled Maeve, 'better men than you would queue up to sleep with me. And I'm wealthier than you. So there!'

'Humph! You're talking through your backside,' grumped Ailill, 'I'm better clothed than you, for starters.' He gazed proudly at the rich garments he'd discarded before climbing into bed.

'You poverty-stricken, pig herder, you,' screeched Maeve in a temper, 'I've more silks, furs, velvets, brocades and fine linens than you any day. You're a pauper compared to me. You're a jumped-up nothing. You'd have sardines for dinner and say you'd had fish.

'My father was the High King of Ireland and had six beautiful daughters. I was the best warrior and the most generous. I mustered a large army long before I met you. My father, the High King, gave me Roscommon, complete with Cruachan, where you now stretch your useless body on my bed.'

'How dare you say I'm lucky while you swan around my property, waited on by my servants, eating my food ... never mind the huge amount you manage to drink. You're lucky I paid any attention to you!'

'Humph!' sneered Ailill. 'You're not the full shilling. You don't appreciate me.'

'You dung beetle,' yelled Maeve, 'I have a high price. You had to pay more to marry me than any other woman in Ireland. And I gave you the width of your face in red gold and the weight of your left arm in light-coloured gold. I repeat, you're useless!'

'You'd be lost without me and you know it!'

'I'm richer than you, better dressed than you, braver than you, cleverer than you–'

'You edjiot, you!' Ailill guldered, 'You don't know your ass from your elbow, I'll larn you, you stupid cow! This hell hole you call home couldn't work without the things I gave you. This place was a dump until you trapped me into marrying you and I brought it a bit of style, I'll show you!'

He shouted for the servants to carry all his household equipment, his iron pots, jugs, buckets, wash pails and so on into the bedchamber and spread them around. 'There,' he demanded proudly, 'look at that!'

'Humph! That's just a few pots and pans. I didn't need your junk; I have my own equipment. Look at these, you oaf, you. I own more than you, so I do.' She called for her servants to fetch her household utensils.

Maeve and Ailill counted their goods and found they had an equal number. Ailill became even more angry.

'What do you think's so great about household junk? How about things with a bit more style, like clothes. I'm better dressed than you. You go around looking like a trollop in rags.'

His servants fetched all his clothes, his silks, furs, linens and cloaks. He watched proudly as they were spread around. He drew himself up his full height and smirked.

'There. Beat that.'

Maeve did likewise and they argued about the relative merits of each item. Eventually they conceded: they were equally well dressed. Maeve's face turned white with rage. Her eyes flashed like emergency beacons in her head.

'Get my jewels, my golden torques, my rubies, my diamonds!' she screeched.

Her servants were terrified. They crept in timidly with jewels, silver trophies and vessels and disappeared as soon as possible.

Looking at her wealth inflamed King Ailill's temper. 'Woman,' he roared, 'you get up my nose! Six eggs to you, and all of them rotten! May your cess go bad.'

He ordered his servants to bring in his valuables, sat back and smirked, 'Look at that! That beats your trash any day! Even an edjiot like you must see my jewels are better than yours!'

'Why are you so proud of a clatter of cheap, tasteless baubles?' sneered Maeve, 'that lot of junk's about as valuable as the pus of a poxy fox in your whiskey.'

'Up yours!' yelled Ailill. 'Look at this diamond. I'll bet you haven't anything as good as that!'

'Shove it up you sideways!' screamed Maeve, producing a diamond of similar quality.

They compared the quality and value of their jewels and again found they had an equal amount. By this time Maeve was fluorescent with rage.

'Where there's muck there's brass,' she screeched as she sent for her herds of animals.

King Ailill yelled at his slaves to round up his animals.

Their slaves were panic-stricken. They knew from experience that their owners' rage could result in them being tortured or murdered. They scoured the countryside rounding up sheep, goats, horses, pigs and cattle.

The couple found they had an equal number of animals, except for one thing. Maeve owned the finest white bull in the whole of Ireland. The bull cast a belligerent eye at Maeve, didn't like what it saw and joined Ailill's animals. That was a serious setback. It

would have been wrong to go against the animal's will, so Maeve felt she had been outclassed and she was devastated. Tradition dictated that in marriage, the partner who owned the most was head of the family. She loathed the idea of being subject to her husband.

She had to find a bull equal to the white one now in King Ailill's herd. She sent for Mac Roth, her messenger, who she knew to be a gossip. He knew everything about everything. He said, 'The chieftain, Dara, a very reasonable sort of bloke, owns a magnificent brown bull, the brown bull of Cooley, equal to the white one in every way. I'm sure if you explain your problem he'd sell his bull. He lives near Dun Dealgan.'

'Wheeker,' exclaimed Maeve, 'tell Dara I'll trade fifty heifers, land, a valuable chariot and a night with me for his bull, so I will.'

Dara was so pleased with Maeve's offer that he bounced up and down on his cushions, making the seams burst open and hordes of feathers scatter into the air.

'Heheheheh,' he giggled, 'I'll play the bull with Maeve. Bull for bull. Heheheh! Thon offer's dead on!'

Mac Roth and his companions were invited into Dara's dun for a feast. They got drunk, became argumentative and began to boast,

'Our queen's a wild woman. If Dara hadn't agreed to sell his bull, she'd have stolen it anyway.'

'What?' exclaimed Dara's men.

'Maeve's a great warrior. Better than Dara. She'd have got thon big bull by fair means or foul. She'd have stolen it if necessary.'

'Queen Maeve and what army?' growled Dara's men.

'Her own army. It's the finest army in the whole of Ireland. We'd knock the melt out of your mingy warriors.'

Dara's men were furious and told Dara what had been said. Dara flew into a temper, sent for Mac Roth and yelled,

'Drink is a curse. It makes you fight with your neighbour. It makes you shoot your enemy and miss. Last night, as I was befuddled with drink. I thought I was being given a decent offer. I was deceived. Tell Queen Maeve she can stay in her own bed and have my bull over my dead body.'

The messengers told Maeve what had happened. She said, 'We needn't polish the knobs and knockers in this. Everyone'd know I'd steal the bull if I had to. To arms! This country is at war!'

She went into her bedchamber, called for a carafe of wine and began to plan a campaign. 'I'll need help,' she thought. 'Ulster's well defended and has that mad dog, that Cúchulainn fella. He'll inspire the Men of Ulster to fight. The other Provinces'll join me if I promise them a share in the spoils. There's no love lost between them and Ulster.'

She gathered a great army which camped around Croachan.

Maeve was determined to show Ailill that she was a great leader. He was amused, but he knew she had a foul temper, so he said nothing. Maeve grew restless as a great army gathered and feverishly consulted sages and druids to determine the best day for setting out to wage war on Ulster. The sages and druids appeared reluctant to name the day.

'Come on, hurry up!' she fumed. 'What's keeping you? You fools! For goodness' sake, conjure up a bit of magic to make an auspicious starting day. The army's ready. Delay's stupid. The men will become restless and want to go home. Forget about omens. It's all superstitious nonsense. Forward I say! Forward! King Conor and the Men of Ulster are suffering labour pains. Thanks to Macha's curse, the men of Ulster suffer labour pains for nine days and nine nights whenever danger threatens the province. The province is undefended except for that mad dog, Cúchulainn. Now's priceless opportunity. To war! *Croachan!*'

She mounted her chariot and asked her charioteer to turn it round to the right to ensure a safe return by drawing down the power of the sun.

A beautiful young girl, dressed in a speckled cloak fastened by a large, shining golden pin suddenly appeared. A richly embroidered hooded tunic framed her delicate features and her sandals were fastened with gold clasps. She sat quietly in her chariot, which was pulled by two black horses and gazed steadily at Maeve with dark troubled eyes. She lifted a slim elegant hand and pushed her hood off her head. She had glorious, golden hair, which was divided into three tresses; two were wound round her head while the third hung down her back. It was so long that it touched her ankles.

The girl's gaze annoyed Maeve.

'Do you want to paint a picture of me?' she snarled.

The girl did not move. Maeve became furious and her eyes began to flash red as she thought, 'Thon wee cow's not scared of me. She's not looking at me with proper respect.'

The girl spoke seriously, 'I am gazing into the future. I do not like what I see.'

'Who do you think you're kidding. The only people who can see the future belong to the Otherworld. Clear away off and take your lying tongue with you.'

'Ahhhhh, that's foolish. My name is Fedelm and I belong to the fairy host living around Rath Cruachan.'

'Well, Fedelm, I suppose I'd better let you have your say. What is going to happen to my mighty army? What spoils of war will we win? What mighty battles?'

'I see crimson. I see red.'

'Your backside. The Men of Ulster are lying in their beds suffering from Macha's curse. I can't lose.'

'Ahhhhhh, I see crimson. I see red.'

'Catch a grip of yourself. I tell you, I can't lose as long as I act
quickly while the Men of Ulster can't get out of their beds. Can't
you see that, you edjiot, you?'

'I see crimson. I see red. Beware!'

'Of course you see crimson and red. Red's the colour of blood.
Wars are bloody. Men spill red blood when they go into battle.
You're a nut case!'

'Beware! I see crimson, red on your army. I see a small man, like
a dragon in battle, doing great deeds of arms. There is a light about
his head. There is victory about his forehead … It is the Hound of
Ulster. Your dead will be many. Women will keen. The memory of
the blood he spills will be everlasting.'

'Augh, for goodness sake, come off it! That's Cúchulainn, the
mad dog of Ulster! I've told you, I can't lose, not unless I follow
advice from headbins like you. I must get going. I can't afford to
wait. The Men of Ulster will recover from their curse and be able
to fight!

'Don't you realise a clatter of King Conor's warriors have joined
my army because they were disgusted with his behaviour. And that
includes King Fergus, Cúchulainn's foster father, and Fergal, the
dog's best friend. Put that in yer pipe and smoke it.'

Maeve ignored Fedelm's advice and set off with her great army.
They crossed the River Shannon north of Lough Ree and travelled
along the road towards Hag's Mountain (Sliabh na Caillighe),
Granard (Granaird), Kells (Cuil) and Dundalk (Dun Dealgan).
Their first night was spent at Kilcooley (Cuil Silinne) in County
Roscommon. Ailill took his place in the middle of the army,
leaving a place for Fergus on his right and one for Maeve on his
left. Maeve herself went off to find out more about the men under
her command, along with Fergus.

'The Men from Leinster are by far the best soldiers. They set up
camp and cooked their food while all the rest of the army had done
was get around to erecting shelters. That's worrying.'

'Why?' asked Fergus.

'They'll claim the victory as their own. We must kill them.'

Fergus was horrified.

'You can't do that!' he gasped. 'No way! It's wrong. I won't stomach it!'

'Stop being such a softy. Why can't we get rid of them? It's a wise move.'

'That's a dishonourable, disgraceful notion. Warriors don't expect to be killed by their own leaders. You owe all the brave warriors who've joined you a debt of gratitude. They are willing to risk their lives for you.'

'Gratitude, my backside! They're in it for a share in the spoils of war,' Maeve replied.

Fergus drew himself to his full height and scowled down at her.

'Kill the Men of Leinster over my dead body and over the dead bodies of my Men from Ulster.'

Maeve flew into a rage and went to strike Fergus with her whip. Then she remembered that she needed his help and used it to tickle him under his chin as she pulled him onto her bed.

'I'll keep him faithful,' she thought. 'The joys of bed are useful, as far as men are concerned. And Fergus is well known for thinking with his balls, not his brains.'

'You big ferocious bear,' she cooed flirtatiously, fluttering her long eyelashes at him, 'how do you expect this little woman to get over her little problem?'

'That's easy. Spread the Leinster warriors among the other troops. That'll strengthen your ranks.'

'Good idea! Your brain is obviously in good working order. I'm sure that's not the only part of you that works,' she said as she pulled him towards and kissed him passionately.

Fergus was astonished. He'd heard Maeve called 'The Queen of Drunkenness', and a rumour that she was a tiger in bed. It must be true; this was real. He responded enthusiastically and Maeve groaned with pleasure. The noise attracted Aillil's attention and he looked in the door. He knew Maeve was simply attempting to enslave Fergus, but ... but, she appeared to be enjoying the process too much. He smiled as he spotted Fergus' sword near the door and quietly removed it.

'Serves him right,' he thought.

Cúchulainn had heard about Maeve's march on Ulster, so he went to Mag Muceda, the Pig Keepers' Plain, felled an oak tree and cut a message, in Ogham, into its trunk: 'Warning. Do not pass until a warrior has leapt over this oak, in his chariot, at the first attempt.'

'That'll learn them,' he muttered as he went to wait and watch.

The great army pitched their tents and some warriors tried to leap the tree. Thirty horses fell. Thirty chariots were smashed. Eventually, Fergus succeeded. Cúchulainn moved in front of the army and threw stones at the warriors with his sling. He killed Maeve's hound, and her pet squirrel, which was perched on her shoulder. He killed Ailill's pet bird and so many warriors died that Ailill yelled, 'We'd better travel by night and day or two thirds of our army will be killed before we find the Brown Bull of Cooley.'

Cúchulainn threw stones which broke limbs and dashed warriors' brains out.

The brown bull had been hidden in a pen on the hillside above Du Largy with nine heifers to keep him company. He felt happy and contented, so sang softly to comfort the Men of Ulster, who were still suffering pain from Macha's curse.

The goddess of war, the Morrigan, turned herself in to a raven and enjoyed the fun. She sat on a standing stone in Tremair Chuailnge and laughed and laughed.

'How can I add to the craic?' she wondered. 'Oh! I know. I'll enrage the brown bull. That should put the cat among the pigeons, so to speak.'

'Get up, you lazy, good for nothing brute, you,' she yelled at the bull, 'What do you think you are? A pussy? Why do you have 100 children playing on your back and 200 Ulster warriors sleeping in your shadow? You're a no-good cissy. Get up and fight the enemy NOW!'

The Brown Bull was incensed. He arose and shook his great head and body; the children fell off and fifty were killed. The bull charged towards the fray, looking for trouble as he ran around and around in ever widening circles.

Cúchulainn stood on the top of Trumpet Hill still throwing stones at Queen Maeve's troops, killing hundreds of men. Her army struggled forwards. It was so large and so heavy that it compacted the ground, making it sink and forming what we now call 'The Windy Gap' in the Cooley Mountains.

The Brown Bull was nowhere to be found so Maeve ordered her warriors to tether their horses among the trees at Faughart. She held a council of war, decided to ask Cúchulainn for a truce and sent a messenger to him. He agreed and arranged to meet a negotiator the following day.

Cúchulainn's charioteer, Laeg, warned Cúchulainn. 'Watch out,' he said, 'Yon Maeve's a big cheat, a sleeked cow, not the sort to want a truce. She'll send warriors to kill you.' Maeve did indeed send warriors to murder Cúchulainn, but he managed to slaughter them all and she began to worry about the number of men Cúchulainn had killed. At first it was easy to find warriors willing to fight Cúchulainn but he killed them all. Eventually no one would volunteer.

Our men'll decide they're on a hiding to nothing and go home,' she moaned.

Ailill suggested they ask Cúchulainn to engage in single combat with a champion from the south. Cúchulainn agreed because it meant he could fight one person at a time rather than the whole army.

Ailill looked thoughtful. 'We'll have to use bribery and to persuade anyone to fight Cúchulainn,' he said. 'Yon daughter of yours, yon Finnabair, she's a real wee cracker. Let's use her as a bribe.'

'Finnabair's a fool. She won't do anything underhand; I'm ashamed of her. She has a sense of honour. I don't know where she got her foolish notions,' Maeve replied.

Ailill suggested that they did not tell Finnabair what they were planning, so they invited her and a likely warrior into their tent and plied them with drink. The warrior was delighted when promised Finnabair's hand in marriage, provided he brought Cúchulainn's head to Maeve. He set out to fight Cúchulainn with a heart filled with hope, but he didn't last five minutes. Cúchulainn slaughtered him.

One day, Cúchulainn was astonished to see a beautiful young woman, wrapped in rich clothes of many colours, coming towards him. She smiled at him. He growled, 'What in the name of all that's wonderful are you doing here? This is a warzone. You could be killed.'

'I've brought you treasure and cattle.'

'You've what? Are you right in the head?'

'I know of your great deeds and am in love with you.'

'I've got more to think of at the moment than a trifle like having some fool woman in love with me. Give my head peace and beat away off.'

The girl's eyes flashed. 'That's no way to talk to me. I'll have your guts for garters.'

'You and what army? Clear off, I said!'

The girl's mood changed and her face became ugly and contorted with hate. 'I'm the Morrigan, the goddess of war. When you fight at the ford, I'll turn into an eel and trip you … I'll cause cattle to stampede and squash you … I'll become a she-wolf and attack you.'

'Wise up. Attack me and I'll smash your ribs with my toes; I'll throw stones and burst your eye. I'll break your legs. You'll never heal unless I bless you and that's the last thing I'd ever do. Clear off, pronto!'

In the meantime, Queen Maeve lay back on her bed, enjoying the feel of its soft furs and silken cushions under her naked body and drank steadily as her eyes flashed red.

'I can't admit my warriors are such wimps that they refuse to fight that beardless dog,' she thought.

She repeated 'beardless dog' to herself and gave a great shout.

'That's it! That's it! Cúchulainn hasn't grown a beard. He has the face of a child. No warrior worth his salt would fight a mere beardless boy. We'll tell him that it wouldn't have been fair to send our best warriors against a mere boy so we sent second-class warriors out, to give him a chance. Loch's an excellent warrior. When Cúchulainn grows a beard, Loch'll fight and kill him!'

Maeve and the women in the camp shouted at Cúchulainn, 'It wouldn't be fair to send a decent warrior against you because you haven't grown a beard. Loch'll fight you when you grow up!'

Cúchulainn was furious. He daubed purple berries around his face and plucked a fistful of long grass at dusk, held it up to his face and shouted through it.

'See! I've grown a beard. Come and fight.'

Loch turned to Queen Maeve and said firmly, 'I'll fight Cúchulainn in seven days' time; not before.'

Maeve's eyes flashed warnings like red headlights.

Loch stared steadily at her. 'If you kill me, you'll have nobody. I need seven days to myself. I've things to do.'

He stared steadily at Maeve, who realising she would have to accept his decision, smiled and said, 'If that's the way it is, it's the way it is.' She thought it would be unwise to give Cúchulainn seven days of rest, so sent a warrior every night to find and kill him. Cúchulainn slaughtered them all.

In desperation, Maeve sneered at Loch.

'Fancy letting that dog, the very one who killed your brother, destroy our army. The dog's just recently grown a beard and you're scared of him. Come and hide behind my skirts. I'll protect you.'

Loch was very annoyed. His face blushed deep scarlet. He remembered how his brother had died and was filled with rage. Grabbing his sword and shield, he strode out, yelling,

'Cúchulainn! Cúchulainn! Come to the ford upstream. Come 'til I kill you!'

Cúchulainn let out a roar that filled every ear with horror. 'Coming!' he yelled, racing towards the ford.

Cúchulainn spotted Loch, stopped momentarily, then leapt towards him, shield and sword flashing in the sunlight. The two men met in ferocious combat in the ford. The Morrigan turned into an eel and wrapped three coils of her long body around Cúchulainn's feet. He stumbled and fell. Loch jumped on him, slashing him with his sword until the water was blood red with gore.

The Men of Ulster looked on in horror, except for one of their number, a warrior called Bricrui, who was jealous of Cúchulainn.

'Haha!' he laughed, 'a little salmon has put you down. You're bleeding like a pig. You're no good, a has-been, you weakling, you.'

Rage surged through Cúchulainn. He rose with a mighty roar, slashed at the eel and smashed its ribs. The commotion caused cattle to stampede. They rushed through Maeve's army, carrying tents off on their horns. The Morrigan turned into a she-wolf and snarled at the cattle, causing them to turn and stampede towards Cúchulainn. He took aim, threw a stone and burst one of her eyes. She then turned into a hornless red heifer and led the cattle dashing through the ford, threatening to trample Cúchulainn into the dirt. He spotted the Morrigan, threw a rock and broke her legs before turning towards Loch and slashing him with his sword. His charioteer, Laeg, threw the *gae bolga* to him. Cúchulainn caught it, examined Loch's body, which was covered in a skin of horn, saw a weak place and screeched, 'Shove this up you sideways!' striking Loch a mortal blow.

Loch screamed, 'Yield to me! Yield to me! Give me space. Give me space to die.'

From that day to this the ford has been called Ath Traigid, the Ford of Yielding.

Cúchulainn stepped back so Loch had room to fall on his face before cutting his head cut off. By this time, Cúchulainn had lost a lot of blood himself and was exhausted. He hid himself among the trees and sat down with his head in his hands.

The Morrigan dragged herself through the undergrowth, gasping in agony.

'I was beautiful,' she moaned, 'Now I'm ugly. I can't bear what he's done to me. My eye looks awful … The hound could fix me if he'd only bless me … but he won't. I'll have to trick him, I can't stay like this … I must think … He's polite … He blesses people when they help him … I really hurt him. Hahaha! He bled like a pig … Hahaha! He's bound to feel weak and thirsty … That's it! It'll require a bit of effort … but it's worth a try. I'll turn into a pathetic old woman milking a cow with three teats. He's bound to ask for a drink.'

She groaned as she changed shape, appearing as a squint-eyed old woman supported by a stick. Cúchulainn raised his head and looked longingly at the cow. He was very thirsty.

'Please spare me some milk?' he pleaded.

The Morrigan was delighted as she squeezed milk from each of the cow's teats.

'Good health to the giver! The blessing of men and gods upon you.'

'Hahaha! Got you!' the Morrigan sneered as she returned to her normal shape.

'Hen's brains and turkey's snatters! If I'd known it was you, I wouldn't have blessed you,' Cúchulainn cried.

Maeve asked Cúchulainn for a truce and suggested they meet to negotiate terms. Laeg smelt a rat.

'Cúchulainn, Maeve's a dirty cheat.' he said. 'She'll set a trap for you.'

'What do you think I should do?' asked Cúchulainn

'Meet her but go armed. Remember, a warrior without his weapons is not under warriors' law. Don't give Maeve a chance to say you were a coward.'

Maeve sent fourteen of her most skilful warriors to ambush Cúchulainn by throwing javelins at him. He killed them all. From that day to this, the place where they fell has been called Focherd, which means the great skill of Cúchulainn.

Cúchulainn became filled with rage at Maeve's treachery and rushed towards her army as it was setting up camp. He killed eight warriors before returning to the woods. Five warriors chased him and he slaughtered them, too.

Fergus realised Maeve and Ailill were not observing the rules of fair play.

'I left the Men of Ulster and King Conor because he was dishonest,' he shouted. 'I've told you before, and I won't tell you again. Play fair and observe the laws of chivalry, or I leave, taking my warriors with me.'

Maeve decided to be prudent. She couldn't afford to lose Fergus, so decided to observe the rules of war. This enabled Cúchulainn to fight one warrior at a time until he reached Trumpet Hill. He rushed up it with a great shout of glee and pelted the invading army with boulders.

Ailill sent for a messenger and said, 'Go and tell Cúchulainn he can marry Finnabair, Maeve's daughter, if he leaves the army alone. I'll bring her to him.'

The messenger duly left and delivered the message. Cúchulainn looked doubtful.

'I don't trust Ailill and Maeve,' he said.

'You have the Alill's word. And he is a king.'

'Yes. Alright, alright. I accept.'

Ailill had no intention of going anywhere near Cúchulainn.

'I'd be stupid to risk my life,' he thought, 'the dog's mad. He'd probably kill me on sight. I've a responsible job here. Maeve needs a good man to curb her excesses.'

'Dress the camp fool like a king, put a crown on his head, then send him to Cúchulainn with Finnabair,' he said. 'The fool can betroth her to Cúchulainn. That should keep him happy until the Men of Ulster recover from the curse and begin the last battle.

The fool took Finnabair towards Cúchulainn and shouted from a distance. 'Cúchulainn, how's about ye? We're lukin' ye.'

Cúchulainn listened carefully and thought.

'That's not Ailill. It's another trick. Ailill would never shout "How's about ye?" He doesn't talk like that.' He approached, knocked the fool's brains out with a stone and rushed up to Finnabair, who trembled as he grabbed her.

'You're more sinned against that sinning,' Cúchulainn snarled. 'I'll spare your life, but I'll teach you a lesson you'll never forget. I'll make you a laughing stock.' He cut off her long hair and stuck a pillar stone up her tunic before impaling the fool on another pillar stone.

Maeve's army camped on Muirthemne Plain, at Breslech Mor.

Cúchulainn forced himself to stay alert, although he was suffering from shock which made him was shiver with cold and exhaustion. He looked up and saw the gold weapons of Maeve's army flickering in the golden glow of the setting sun and the sight filled him with rage. He opened his mouth wide and uttered a terrible warrior's scream that came from deep within his being. His hideous battle cry made demons, devils and goblins reply. The awful sounds reverberated though the still air so much that Queen Maeve's soldiers trembled in panic and a hundred dropped dead with fright.

Laeg felt very sorry for Cúchulainn. He stood up and watched, ready to warn him of danger. 'Cú,' he said, 'there's a man coming towards us.'

'What kind of a man?'

'He's tall and broad with short curly fair hair. He has a green cloak fastened by a large silver broach and a red knee-length tunic of silk embroidered in red gold. He's got a black shield with a knob of light gold on it. He's carrying a five-pointed spear and a forked javelin. That's odd. Nobody's paying the slightest attention to him. I don't think they can see him.'

Cúchulainn breathed a sigh of relief. 'The Shee know I'm struggling alone, defending Ulster and at the end of my tether,' he said, 'they've sent help.'

The warrior reached Cúchulainn, smiled and said, 'Son, I'm proud of you. But you're wounded and exhausted.'

'Who are you?'

'I'm your father, the sun god Lugh. Your mother sends her love. I'm going to help you. Now, let's have a look at those wounds. Relax. I'll look after things for three days and three nights so you can rest. You've haven't had any sleep for ages.'

'I'm alright, Dad. I've snatched a few moments shut-eye here and there.

Lugh smiled. 'Come on, son. You need a proper rest. Let's go to the Death Mound of Du Largy. It's dry and quiet in the inner chamber. You can relax safely there while I take care of things for you.'

Cúchulainn staggered into the Death Mound of Du Largy's inner chamber, lay down and said, 'Thank you. This is a good place. If I die here, I'll go straight to the Otherworld once the sun focuses on my body at the Winter Solstice.'

Lugh laughed, 'You're not ready to go to the Otherworld, not yet. You've other mighty deeds to do.' He examined and cleaned Cúchulainn's wounds with herbs and grasses so they healed as he rested.

Cúchulainn slept soundly. When he woke he saw his father,

'I could sit up and eat an egg,' he said. 'How long have I slept?'

'Three days and three nights.'

'Wow, that's awful!'

'Why do you say that?'

'Maeve's army will have regrouped.'

'No they haven't. The Boys' Brigade came to help. They were outnumbered but managed to kill three times their number before the last one was slaughtered.'

Cúchulainn groaned. 'Those were Ulster's best boy soldiers. If I hadn't slept they would still be alive.'

'You're talking through your left ear. You should be happy for them. They'll go straight to the Otherworld. Life's hard and they've escaped. They'll never have to cope with being old and stiff and in pain. Come on. Cheer up.'

'Come father, let's avenge the death of the boys.'

'No. That would be foolish. I don't want history crediting me with your great deeds. Maeve's army has no power over your life, so go alone and get the credit. That way you'll gain your life's ambition, to live a life that is remembered.'

Cúchulainn asked Laeg to prepare his chariot, grabbed his weapons and cast a spell, throwing a circle around the four great provinces of Ireland. He gave a loud battle cry and killed so many of his enemies that it was impossible to count their bodies. Laeg and he did not suffer a scratch. Cúchulainn felt proud of his great deeds and wanted to show off. He put on his purple mantle and fastened it with a brooch of light-gold and silver inlaid with gold. He donned his warrior apron made of dark red royal silk and carried his crimson shield decorated with gold. His sword had a gold hilt and an ivory guard. Laeg put his gold riveted javelin into his chariot. He lifted nine human heads in one hand, ten in the other, and shook them at his enemies. His thick hair that was yellow at the crown, red in the middle and brown at the end. The women became curious and asked their husbands to let them climb up on their shields so they could watch. They were very impressed with what they saw. Queen Maeve, however, hid under her shield because she thought if Cúchulainn saw her he'd throw a stone and kill her. She tried not to tremble at the thought.

That night, Queen Maeve's army camped at the great stone of Ross, where she failed to find a volunteer to go and fight Cúchulainn. She ordered Fergus to go and fight first thing next day.

Fergus refused. 'That's unreasonable. I won't fight my foster son.'

Maeve laughed 'I didn't ask you to leave King Conor. Surely you realised when you joined my army that you'd have to fight your own sort? Maybe you just left so you could hide behind my skirts and whimper. You're nothing but a scaredy cat. I thought you were a tiger, but you're nothing but a pussy. Here puss, puss, puss!'

Fergus turned crimson with embarrassment, but picked up his weapons and went towards Cúchulainn. King Ailill smirked – he still had Fergus's sword.

Cúchulainn was horrified to see Fergus at the ford. 'Master,' he said, 'I don't want to fight you. It's not fair. You haven't got your sword.'

Fergus smiled and said, 'Could we make a bargain? I had to come because that she-wolf called me a pussy. I'd have been a laughing stock if I'd stayed. Will you save my face and give way to me? I promise, during the last fight I'll run away and the Men of Ireland will follow. If you don't want a bargain kill me now, quickly.'

Cúchulainn agreed the bargain. Laeg prepared his chariot and they acted out a fierce fight until Cúchulainn turned and began to run away.

'Kill him! Kill him!' yelled Maeve. 'Don't let the dog escape.'

'No, I won't. I've done more than any other of your warriors. And I won't attack him again until all the Men of Ireland have fought him single-handed. So there.'

So, Maeve went to Ferdia, Cúchulainn's best friend.

'Ferdia, you trained with Cúchulainn. You know how his mind works. It's up to you to win this battle. Go out and fight.'

'No. He's my friend.'

'I'll give you land. Anything you want.'

'No, no, NO. I won't fight Cúchulainn for anything. Not for the sun, moon and stars.'

Maeve turned to her courtiers and said, 'He's scared. Cúchulainn said the first time Ferdia faced him, he'd fall.'

'He'd no right to say that. I swear … if he really did say such a thing, I'd fight him tomorrow.'

'He did. You have my word on it.'

'Then I'll fight him tomorrow.'

'That's more like it.'

The next day Ferdia got up early and waited by the ford for Cúchulainn. They were very evenly matched, each returning wounded to camp, having agreed to meet again next day.

The following day they fought until they were exhausted.

'Ferdia, I'm knackered.'

'So am I.'

'Let's stop this nonsense and agree to start again in the morning.'

'Good idea.' Ferdia threw his weapons on the ground. Cúchulainn did likewise and they hugged before returning to their camps.

Queen Maeve jeered at Ferdia. 'You and your friend are playing games, behaving like a young trainee warrior having mock fights. Kill the enemy. Come back tomorrow with Cúchulainn's head or I'll take drastic action against you.'

The next day, the fight between Ferdia and Cúchulainn was deadly. Both men were wounded. Then Ferdia caught Cúchulainn off guard and hit him hard with the blade of his sword, turning the water of the ford red with blood. Cúchulainn yelled to Laeg to throw him his special spear, *gae bolga*, which he caught with his feet and threw at Ferdia. It passed straight through Ferdia's shield into his chest and ended up with the point sticking out through his back.

Ferdia groaned, 'OHHHHHHhhhhhhhhhhhhh you've killed me.'

Cúchulainn ran to Ferdia, picked him up and carried him over to the north side of the river, so that his body would be with the Men of Ulster, not the Men of Ireland. He cradled Ferdia in his arms and sobbed bitterly.

The Men of Ulster recovered from Macha's curse, came to join the battle and attempted to comfort Cúchulainn as he removed his *gae bolga* from Ferdia's body. Cúchulainn, still weeping bitterly, was gently led away from the scene to the five streams of Conaille Muirthemne. The Shee threw healing herbs into the water, making them green with leaves. A town, now known as Ardee, developed around the ford where Ferdia died.

King Conor arrived and the Men of Ulster marched on Maeve's army in a battle that raged throughout Ireland. Maeve began to feel very uncomfortable on Knocknaree Mountain in County Sligo.

'I can't,' she thought, 'not here, not now!' But the feeling became urgent. She turned to her husband and said, 'Husband, I need a pee.'

Ailill looked at her in amazement. 'You can't need a pee. Not in the middle of a battle. Not here!'

'If you've got to go, you've got to go,' she snarled as she climbed down from her chariot and disappeared behind a bush. Three streams rushed from her as her bowels burst open.

Just then, Cúchulainn caught sight of Maeve. He felt his anger rage up his gullet as he rushed behind the bush, saw what she was doing and roared with laughter. He lowered his sword and said, 'It wouldn't be fair to kill you now.'

From that day to this, the place is known as 'The Place of Queen Maeve's Foul Deed'.

Queen Maeve sent eight messengers to find the Brown Bull and his heifers. 'Whatever happens, the Brown Bull must come home with me to Croachan. Find it immediately,' she ordered.

The Brown Bull had left Ulster and headed south. On reaching Connaught, he bellowed with rage. The White Bull heard him, became furious, escaped and raced towards the sound. The bulls' eyes bulged out of their heads like balls of fire when they saw each other. They pawed the ground, sending sods of earth flying through the air as they locked horns in battle. The Men of Ireland trembled as they listened to the noise. The bulls fought all night. At dawn, the Brown Bull appeared in the west, carrying the remains of the White Bull stuck on his horns. Maeve's sons rushed out to kill him to revenge the death of the White Bull but Fergus stopped them.

'Let the Brown Bull go back to his own country,' he commanded.

The Brown Bull bellowed three times, then set off home. He stopped to drink at the ford of the Sionnan. Two of the White Bull's loins fell into the water there, so the place is called Ath-luin or Athlone, the ford of the loin.

He had another drink from a river in Meath where the White Bull's liver fell off. That place became known as Ath Truim (Trim), the place of the liver.

When he reached the top of Slieve Breagh and caught sight of his own country, the Brown Bull rushed on, killing everyone who got in his way. He gave a great bellow of victory when he reached Druim Tairb, his great heart burst and he dropped dead. Druim Tairb, the Ridge of the Bull, was named after him.

Both bulls had died in battle so Ailill and Maeve felt there was no point in further fighting. They made peace with the Men of Ulster and returned home to Croachan.

9

THE DEATH OF CONLA
AT ROSNAREE

Tom McDevitte told me this story as we stood in the graveyard belonging to the Anglican church overlooking Rosnaree. When he finished the story, he took me to a quiet corner near the back of the church. Tears streamed down Tom's old face as he pointed at a grave and said, 'Doreen, you must think me a silly old man but I too lost a child. My wee daughter was two years of age. She was playing in her wee playpen beside me, in front of an electric fire. I was reading the paper and dropped a few pages on the floor. I didn't notice her pick a page up and poke it into the fire. She was badly burnt and died a few days later. I have fine sons but she was my only daughter.'

There was a terrible commotion outside Cúchulainn's home at Dun Dealgan. Cúchulainn's first thought was that his home was being attacked. He leapt out of bed and grabbed his weapons as he rushed to the doorway. But instead of the armed warriors he was expecting, he found an excited, unarmed crowd outside

'What what are you jabbering about?' he asked the excited crowd, 'I had a rough night and was enjoying a peaceful bit of shut-eye.'

'There's a wee lad, who's just arrived on Rosnaree Strand. He says he's from Skye and that you're a cissy and he challenges you to a fight,' was the quick reply.

Cúchulainn's heart lurched. Skye and Skya. He remembered them both and his advanced warrior training. Skya was some woman, some warrior. He'd never met the like. He remembered the wild, red hair curling around her face, her muscular body, her strength, the smell of danger that hung around her, the way she moved like a tiger. He gasped with admiration as he remembered how she had had one breast cut off because it interfered with her aim when she used her bow and arrow. He had both feared and loved her. She had a formidable reputation. She killed fresh young warriors on sight unless they managed to prove their ability in combat.

He had decided to go to Skya for advanced warrior training because her school had the reputation of being the best in the world and he was determined to be the greatest warrior in creation.

He'd found Skya's fort set into a cliff, protected by a drawbridge over a yawning chasm. He had stayed hidden, watching and waiting. Eventually a young warrior had come along.

'Skya,' he'd guldered, 'I've come to join your army. I'm a great warrior. Let me in.'

Immediately a hundred warriors had appeared at the battlements and began shooting arrows and throwing missiles. The young warrior was hit and fell to his death in the abyss below.

A second warrior appeared. He'd seen what had happened and waited until Skya's soldiers had disappeared, then started to run over the bridge. He got about halfway across before it collapsed. He screamed as he fell to the jagged rocks below.

'Nothing ventured, nothing gained,' thought Cúchulainn. 'I must stop behaving like a big girl's blouse and go into action. When the going gets tough the tough get going. Now let me think. I obviously shouldn't announce my presence ... Or should I? Skya won't enrol new applicants for warrior training unless they prove themselves ... Tell you what. I'll announce my presence, but stand well out of arrow range. That way I can shout insults ... but what next? How do I get in? There's no point in calmly walking over the drawbridge. It's rigged to collapse … I could bounce on it and do my salmon leap over the wall … Here's hoping … Nothing ventured, nothing gained. Here goes.'

He stood well back and yelled, 'Hey Skya. I'm Cúchulainn. I'm the Hound of Ulster. I want to join your warrior school.'

Warriors appeared immediately, peered over the parapet and began shooting arrows. Cúchulainn laughed and laughed as the arrows struck the ground in front of him.

'Call yerselves marksmen?' he jeered, 'Ye couldn't hit a cow up the ass with a bake board! Come on! Come on! Ye must crack the nut before ye can eat the kernel. Ye haven't the strength to reach me. Yer bum's out the door!'

He made rude signs as he stood jeering and laughing, waiting for his attackers to run out of arrows, or tire. When the flow of arrows ceased, he gave a loud yell and rushed towards the bridge, gave a mighty jump, bounced on the middle then leapt like a salmon over the walls and landed inside Skya's fort. He gasped as he glanced around. The warriors were standing well back. The fiercest woman he had ever seen stood in the middle of the compound. She snarled as she unsheathed a dagger. 'So ye want to fight, do ye?'

She leapt towards him. Cúchulainn drew his dagger and circled her. She jumped forward and thrust at him. He avoided her blade and they began to fight in earnest. Their battle lasted for hours; it was dusk when Skya managed to trip Cúchulainn and leap on his chest, pinning him to the ground. She held a dagger to his throat.

'You fight well,' she snarled, 'so I'll spare your life, but I'll put you under a *geassa*. If I ever need you, you must return to me or be cursed forever. Now come on. Fighting makes me randy.' She grabbed his arm and pulled him into her bedchamber.

Cúchulainn enjoyed his warrior training and being with Skya but eventually felt he had to go back to Ireland. He had responsibilities there. Skya was heartbroken at the idea of losing her lover – she was expecting his baby. Cúchulainn did his best to comfort her but insisted he had to return home. He gave her his ring and said, 'When our son is old enough to have warrior training, give him this ring and send him to me.'

Skya agreed and gave him his *gae bolga*, that wonderful spear that had saved his life so many times. Cúchulainn gave a big sigh. He had so many happy memories of his time on Skye; he didn't want to fight anyone from there.

'What age do you say the wee lad is?' he asked.

'He looks about seven years.'

'Well tell him I've no desire to fight weans.'

'He said you'd make that excuse. He says you're no' the full whack, a head banger who's scared to fight. He said you've been too old to fight for years and have a big yellow streak up the centre of your back.' The crowd began to laugh.

Cúchulainn saw that if he didn't at least talk to the intruder he was going to be branded a coward. Reluctantly, he donned on his full warrior gear and hastened down to the shore. There he saw a small boy jumping up and down and brandishing a sword.

'Are you the great Cúchulainn?' he yelled, 'Come and fight.'

'I don't fight mere children. Don't be foolish. Put your sword away and come and join me for a bite to eat.'

'You're scared to fight.'

'I'm not scared. I only fight people my own size.'

'Scaredy custard,' yelled the child. 'Come and fight. You're chicken.'

He jumped through the air, landed at Cúchulainn's feet and kicked his shins before attempting to draw blood with his sword. Cúchulainn was mortified as the crowd laughed. He had to defend himself. The two opponents circled round each other. Cúchulainn felt puzzled. He could swear blind he had never seen the boy before but he looked strangely familiar. Who was he like? Where had he learnt to fight like that? Eventually Cúchulainn tripped the lad, landed on top of him and held his dagger to the boy's throat in an attempt to treat him as he had been treated by Skya so many years ago. Unfortunately the boy lunged upwards and the artery in his neck was severed. As the blood gushed out, he put his hand out and showed Cúchulainn a ring, the very ring he'd given Skya all those years ago and said, 'I'm your son, Conla. This is my mother's ring. She said to give it to you and to remind you she has you under a *geassa*. She needs you. She is being attacked by a tribe of small brown men. You must go to her or be cursed for evermore.' With that, he died.

Cúchulainn was horrified. He had accidentally killed his only son. He cradled the boy's lifeless body in his arms and wept bitterly before taking his warriors across to Skye to defend Skya.

10

KING BRIAN BORU'S TALKATIVE TOES

I got this story from one of the greatest storytellers Ireland has ever produced, John Campbell, who lived in Mullabawn. He said he got it off his mother who got it – when she was young – off her neighbour, the poet Patrick Kavanagh. I suspect John changed the story slightly as it is full of anachronisms, but as it's so much fun, who cares? I once had the pleasure of hearing him telling this story to children. He used it to underline the fact that we tend to take the different parts of our bodies very much for granted until they stop working.

King Brian Boru was the grandson of St Lorcan, the patron saint of Omeath. He was born in the year AD 941 and died at the Battle of Clontarf on 23 April 1014. He was the High King of Ireland and that, as you can imagine, was a very stressful job. Early one morning he felt so tired that he turned to his wife, Queenie (he called her 'Queenie' because as his wife she was the High Queen of Ireland) and said, 'Queenie, I'm soooooooooo tired, I can hardly get out of bed.'

'God love ye, Brian,' said Queenie, 'sure haven't ye been having a hard time lately. Being the High King of Ireland is no picnic for a job. Sure, you can have a wee bit of a lie in while I go downstairs and make you a big fry-up for yer breakfast.'

'Queenie,' said Brian, 'It's at moments like these I know why I had the sense to marry ye.'

Queenie climbed out of bed, put on her green wellington boots and clattered down the castle's staircase into the kitchen. She took her frying pan off the shelf, put a good dollop of lard in it and fried six rashers of bacon, twelve pork sausages, three fresh eggs, four pancakes, five pieces of soda bread, five pieces of potato bread and a handful of mushrooms. He had a good appetite, had King Brian Boru.

King Brian Boru lay in bed, enjoying the smell of bacon drifting up the stairs. Sure, isn't it a wonderful thing to be lying in bed, smelling bacon frying?

Queenie finished cooking and let a big gulder out of her. 'BRIAN! COME DOWN FOR YER BREAKFAST!'

'COMING, QUEENIE!' shouted Brian, throwing back the bedclothes.

In those days the bedclothes were not like ours. Duvets had not been invented. King Brian Boru was wealthy so had fine linen sheets and furs made from wolf skins. Ireland was overrun with wolves in those days. They were a nuisance, gobbling up sheep and children, so it was a very good idea to make them into bed coverings. Their fur was lovely and soft.

As Brian threw back the bedclothes his right big toe spoke to him. 'It's a fine feisty morning, Brian,' it said.

Brian couldn't believe his ears, then his left big toe spoke. 'It is that.'

Brian was terrified. He thought he was going crazy.

'I knew I was stressed,' he muttered, 'but I didn't realise I was going stark, staring bonkers. Toes can't talk to you! Perhaps being High King of the whole of Ireland is too hard a job for me to hold down. Perhaps I should abdicate? Perish the thought.'

He lay and shivered under his wolf skins then he got to thinking. 'I'm an excellent High King. People are happy under my rule. I must remember I am the High King of the whole of Ireland. A High King should be frightened of nothing, never mind his own two feet. I must be brave and act with dignity.'

He sat up in bed and pulled his golden crown with its gleaming jewels straight on his head. (He was very proud of his position and never went to bed without his crown. He was a little bit pompous, was King Brian Boru.) Throwing back the bedclothes, he glowered at his feet.

'We were talking, Brian,' said the left toe.

'I heard you. Why were you talking?'

'We're fed up inside your smelly socks. We want to go home.'

'My socks are NOT smelly.'

'Oh, yes, they are. They're stinking.'

'They can't be,' replied Brian, 'I'm a very clean king. I make a point of having a bath once a year.'

'That's beside the point,' said the right toe, 'bath or no bath, your socks are smelly and we want to go home.'

'I don't see how you can go home. You're stuck on my feet and anyway, I need you.'

'Look Brian, ye know nothin',' replied the right toe, 'Ye've five toes on your right foot and five toes on your left foot. Five and five's ten. That's greedy. It's too many toes. You wouldn't even miss us if you let us go home. And don't ye know, if you pull your toes really hard they come off like lego and ye can stick them back on again.'

'Go on,' said the left toe, 'Give it a go. Try pulling us off and let us go home.'

King Brian Boru began to think and think and think. It was a slow process because he was better at fighting than thinking. He thought seriously about his two big toes. If he had to get up in the middle of the night to visit the bathroom what did he hit against the furniture? His big toe. When he danced a jig with Queenie and she leapt into the air in her green wellies, what did she land on? His big toe. Hitting his toe against the furniture hurt, and so did Queenie. She was a big, fat, heavy woman. It's not pleasant thing to have a heavyweight land on your toe and Queenie lived in the days when fat was a status symbol. Ordinary people could not afford enough food, so were thin. Queenie was the High Queen of the whole of Ireland and the wife of a rich monarch. She could have as much food as she could eat. As a result, she was the fattest woman in the whole of Ireland. When she jumped on Brian's big toe, it hurt like crazy so King Brian Boru began to think he would be better off without his big toes. They appeared to know what he was thinking because they yelled, 'Come on, Brian. Be a sport. Do us a favour. Pull us off and let us go home. Come on, be a sport. Let's go home.'

King Brian Boru bent down and absentmindedly pulled his toes off. They came away from his feet very easily. The minute they were free they each grew two little legs and a pair of arms and shouted, 'Hi! Thanks a bucket, Brian. Ye're dead on,' as they dashed out the bedroom door.

Queenie let another big gulder out of her. 'COME ON, BRIAN! YER EGGS ARE GETTING A SKIN ON THEM. YE KNOW YE DON'T LIKE THEM THAT WAY. COME DOWN FOR YER BREAKFAST!'

'COMING, QUEENIE!' guldered Brian as he stepped out of bed and attempted to rush out of the bedroom. He fell flat on his face. He'd lost his toes and toes are needed for balance.

Queenie heard the thump and immediately thought, 'Brian's dropped dead. He's had a heart attack.' She rushed up the stairs shouting, 'Brian! Brian! Are you alright, Brian? Are you alright?'

She found him sitting on the floor sobbing, 'I've lost my toes, Queenie. I've lost my toes. I can't walk because I've lost my toes. I'll never be able to fight again. I've lost my big toes.'

'Nonsense,' said Queenie, who was a very sensible woman. 'You can't have lost your toes. People don't lose toes.'

'Look,' said Brain pointing at his feet.

'That was very careless of you, Brian, imagine losing yer toes What happened to them? Where are they?'

'I don't rightly know. They ran out the door.'

'Well, I suppose I'd better go and find them.'

Queenie rushed out of the bedroom door, down the stairs, through the kitchen, across the courtyard, over the drawbridge and down the road. She was a big fat woman, the biggest and fattest woman in the whole of Ireland, so she couldn't run very fast. All her fat bounced up and down while she was trying to move forwards and it kept her back. It was as well buses hadn't been invented at that time, because she'd never have been able to run and catch one. She'd be running still if the toes hadn't stopped in the middle of the road to have a fight. They couldn't remember which was the right toe and which was the left toe and were knocking the melt out of each other.

'I'm the right toe,' yelled the left toe, thumping the living daylights out of right toe.

'No ye're not, I'm the right toe. I'm the right toe!' yelled the right toe as it thumped the left toe in return.

'I'm the right toe!'

'No! I am!'

The fight went on and on. Queenie stood in the middle of the road and wondered what she should do. If she went to pick the toes up, they would probably run away. They could run in two different directions and she'd never catch them. Worse still, they could run into a field of oats and it would be impossible to see, never mind catch them. 'I'll have to be crafty,' thought Queenie, looking down at the toes.

'What gives with you guys?' she asked. 'Why are you fighting in the middle of the road?'

'We can't remember who's the right toe and who's the left toe!' the toes shouted together.

'Well, fighting about it isn't going to solve the problem. Why don't you go and ask Brian? He's sure to know who's who. He's a quare decent fella. I'm sure he'd tell you.'

'Good thinking, woman,' shouted the toes as they turned and ran back up the road, over the drawbridge, across the courtyard, through the kitchen, up the stairs and into Brian's bedroom.

'Brian! Brian! Brian!' they shouted, 'Which one's the right toe? Which one's the right toe?'

'Come here till I have a good look at you toes. I can't tell unless I can see you clearly. My eyesight isn't as good as it once was.'

The toes went over to Brian. He bent down and picked them up. 'There,' he said, sticking the right toe back on his foot. 'There. You're the right toe. And you're the left toe.' With that, he stuck the left toe back in position.

'Ta! Ta! Thanks,' yelled the toes. 'Now we know who's who, pull us off again and let's go home.'

'I can't do that, toes,' said Brian, 'I'm sorry, but I need you, toes. I can't walk without you, toes. You'll just have to live in my smelly socks, but I'll tell you what I'll do. I'll have a bath twice a year.'

From that day until the day he was killed at the Battle of Clontarf, in the year 1014 along with his son and his grandson, King Brian Boru had to sleep with his socks on to stop his toes talking to each other and keeping him awake.

If you have to sleep with your socks on, it goes to show that you're descended from King Brian Boru, the High King of the whole of Ireland and one of the greatest kings the world has ever known. It's a crying shame that after the Battle of Clontarf, one of the fleeing Vikings stumbled across his tent, burst in and beheaded him. His body was put in a coffin and carried all the way to Armagh. The pallbearers, who took it across the ford at Oldbridge, could not have guessed that over 600 years later, this would be the site of a famous battle, the Battle of the Boyne.

Brian's sad cortège travelled up Rath Hill and on into Ulster, where his body was buried in the grounds of what is now the Anglican cathedral in the city of Armagh.

11

THE CROW (PREACHAN) OF OMEATH

She was an old, old woman, with an old woman's wrinkled face covered in the brown blotches of age. Her hair was sparse and wispy and she had the long pointed nose of a witch. Yet although she was old and frail, her eyes were bright and inquisitive. She had been born nosey. She loved to know everyone's business.

The old woman lived in the townland of Knocknagoran, one of the ten townlands of Omeath, and some said she was at least 250 years of age.

The next oldest person around Omeath was 92. She remembered the old, old woman when she was a child and the old, old woman was old even then. Some people said she was a witch, others said she had no right to live that length of time and everybody said she was very annoying. She spent her days leaning across her old stone wall shouting at passers by,

'*Ca bhfuil sibh ag dul?*' (Where are you going then?)

This was in the days before public transport and nobody was ever going anywhere far away, or doing anything very interesting. There is one sure thing, though: if anybody had been doing anything out of the ordinary in the ten townlands around Omeath, everybody would have known about it. There was no need to ask, yet if you passed the old woman a hundred times in the day she would shout, '*Ca bhfuil sibh ag dul?*'

Some people always answered truthfully, thinking she was a witch who would put a curse on them if they lied. Other, bolder souls, gave a different answer every time. One day, a crowd of leprechauns passed the old woman after dark. She should been inside at that time of the night, not out by her wall as usual.

'*Ca bhfuil sibh ag dul?*' she asked the leprechauns.

'To the fairy fort above Ardaghy.'

'*Ca bhfuil sibh ag ansin?*' (Where are you going now?)

'We are going to dance with the fairies.'

'*Ca bhfuil sibh ag dul?*' (Where are you going then?)

'Back home to our souterrain under the mountains.'

'*Ca bhfuil sibh ag dul?*'

'Ca, Ca, Ca, Ca, Ca, Ca! Can you not say anything apart from Ca, Ca, Ca!' shouted one of the leprechauns, who was fed up with her continual questioning and was in a rage.

'Ca, Ca, Ca! That's all you can say. Ca, Ca, Ca. You don't deserve to have human form. Ca, Ca, Ca!' And with that he turned her into a crow. She can still be seen today, on her wall, or strutting up and down shouting, 'Ca, Ca, Ca!'

12

THE BIG WIND

For a time, I was seconded to the Ulster Folk and Transport Museum, and Dr Jonathan Bell got me interested in 'The Big Wind'. He suggested I contact Peter Carr, who has done a lot of research on the subject and written an excellent book, *The Big Wind*, published by White Row Press, 1991. Peter could not have been more helpful and thanks are due to both.

On 6 January 1839, a terrible gale swept through the whole of Ireland. It was so awful that people used to date their lives as 'before the Big Wind' or 'after the Big Wind'.

On 8 January, the *Dublin Evening Post* commented, 'The annals of Ireland do not furnish anything in the remotest degree parallel to this hurricane – nor has there ever been a visitation in this country attended with more tremendous, extensive and calamitous consequences.'

There was extensive damage throughout the country and County Louth was no exception. The roof of Mr McCann's house on the Drogheda Quays was destroyed when some chimney stacks fell on it. Drogheda's Mayoralty House had its roof partially blown off. Ships in the harbour were badly damaged; the brigs *Commerce*, *Joannes*, *Anna* and *Thomas & Nancy* had their masts blown down and their bulwarks and timbers damaged. The sloop *Endeavour*, which was from Drogheda, was laden with coals at the time and it sank at Liverpool. Two of the crew were drowned.

Dundalk was wrecked by the storm. Most of the houses and public buildings had roofs blown off and windows blown in. The chimneys from the post office in Earl Street fell through the roof and crashed through all the floors and into the kitchen. The unfortunate postman and his clerk, who were waiting for the mail coach to arrive, were badly injured by the tumbling chimney, which knocked them through the floor and into the cellar below. Houses were left open to the sky, bricks, timbers and slates were scattered in all directions. Huge trees were uprooted and many inhabitants were made homeless.

Many poverty-stricken people lived in dwellings referred to as cabins. They were built from sods of earth stacked on top of each other and thatched with any material that happened to be at hand, such as heather, gorse, grass and so on. These cabins were heated by a fire in the middle of the dwelling, which was also used for cooking. A hole in the roof allowed smoke out. They didn't have any windows or doors; people went in and out through a hole in the wall against which they propped a screen made of willow branches in an attempt to keep the draft out.

Cabins were found on the edge of cities, towns, villages and hamlets. They were very fragile structures with a life span of approximately ten years. As they aged, their desperate owners did their best to prolong their dwellings' lives by propping the walls up with branches of trees, as cabins had a tendency to collapse and kill or maim people unfortunate enough to be inside. The Big Wind caused many of the cabins to collapse or catch fire, so in one dreadful night, thousands of people became homeless.

The majority of Irish birds were blown away and doubtless perished. It took years for the bird population to recover. Folklore associated with the Big Wind is interesting because of the human characteristic to connect cause and effect. Science, as we know it, was in its infancy in 1839 and lack of knowledge gives rise to superstition.

The brutality and violence of the storm shocked and horrified

people living in Ireland at the time. They compared it to a 'West Indian hurricane', or a 'tornado'. The intelligentsia found it intellectually as well as physically shocking. They, like those in the rest of Europe, were excited and dazzled by recent advances in the science. For the first time, it was felt that nature could be controlled. After all, wolves had been exterminated in Ireland, the primal forest had been felled and vast areas of bog and waste had been changed into fields, canals, and roads. Steam engines had been invented, giving rise to rail travel, and steam itself was in the process of making wind power obsolete at sea. Nothing seemed impossible and it appeared as if nature could be taken for granted. That is why the storm came as such a shock. Nature unexpectedly humbled the landscape and human self-confidence was momentarily shaken.

The timing of the storm was seen to be significant. It occurred on the night of Epiphany. Epiphany means the enlightenment that occurred when the three wise men brought presents to baby Jesus. Folklore says that they visit Ireland on the anniversary of that event. This Christian celebration can be traced back to the ancient pagan festival which it replaced, a festival associated with death divination, when the living believed the dead came very close to their loved ones. Lady Jane Wilde (Oscar Wilde's mother) wrote: 'On Twelfth Night, the dead walk, and on every tile of the house a soul is sitting waiting for your prayers to take it out of purgatory.'

The storm arrived on Sunday and reached its height on Monday, the day traditionally associated with Judgement Day in Gaelic Ireland. That greatly added to its significance, as far as the Irish were concerned.

The morning of Sunday 6 January had been beautiful; the land was covered in the previous night's heavy snowfall. The sun rose about 8.30 a.m. and children rushed out to make snowballs and snowmen. The day was so calm that two vessels that had sailed out from Cobh had to anchor because there was 'scarcely any wind'. The tranquillity of the morning was almost unearthly. West of County Louth, in Westmeath, Thomas Russell recalled the Big wind by writing:

> So appalling was the calm that the sensitive flame of a rush candle burned in the open air without the faintest attempt to flicker, and so awe-inspiring was the stillness that prevailed that voices in ordinary conversational tones floated to and fro between farmhouses more than a mile apart. There was something awful in the dark stillness of that winter day, for there was no sunlight coming through the thick, motionless clouds that hung over the earth.

It began to get very warm during the afternoon. A temperature rise of 10°F was recorded south of County Louth, in Phoenix Park, Dublin. The temperature rise was even greater further north, in Belfast. Mrs Francis Howard, wife of the vicar of Swords later wrote, 'the night was very calm and hot, the air felt like the air in a hothouse'.

The only people who guessed a huge storm was gathering were those who happened to read a barometer. A householder, in Limerick noticed that the glass 'shewed quicksliver (mercury) under the extreme lowest mark.'

A deep depression had formed in the Western Atlantic and the Big Wind was caused by a rapid change from warm to cold air. A light westerly breeze blew up about 9 p.m. and grew steadily stronger until it turned into a destructive tempest. People heard a rumbling noise, like thunder, followed by a rushing blast of very strong wind, which shook houses so much that delft and glasses were thrown from their shelves. Houses appeared to rock or tremble on their foundations and slates were plucked off roofs like feathers off Christmas turkeys.

The effect of the Big Wind was so devastating that it has passed into folklore and many people at the time thought God was passing judgement on the Irish for some wrongdoing.

13

THE LONG WOMAN'S GRAVE

In the past I lectured on Irish Folklore in the Department of Continuing Education at Queen's University Belfast. I think I learnt much more from my students than they ever did from me. I got this tale from a student whose name I unfortunately cannot remember, but to whom I am very grateful.

Omeath's celebration of the Feast of St Lorcan, of Cille-Cam, occurs on 10 August and takes the form of a Pattern Day, a mixture of religious celebration and fun. Saint Lorcan was the grandfather of the greatest High King Ireland has ever known, King Brian Boru, and like his illustrious ancestor, he was a great fighter.

Once the 'rounds' had been done, the people set off to enjoy themselves and the craic was mighty. A street of tents was set up in a field, selling of all kinds of refreshment while a great tent, called a rinka, was erected for dancers. Outside on the green, the *Rinceadh Fadha*, or Long Dance, was performed. It's a very ancient set of steps, similar to that danced in the East over 1,000 years ago, and it's said to show the origin of the Celts. At the end of the day, engaged couples from the ten townlands around Omeath walked up the mountain road to the Long Woman's Grave beside the Bog of Anenagh. There each couple picked up a stone and cast it on the grave.

The story of the Long Woman's Grave, also called the Cairn of Cauthleen, begins with Conn O'Hanlon, an ancient chief of the district.

Conn O'Hanlon had two sons, whom he loved dearly and wanted to treat equally. His eldest son, also called Conn, was a lad who liked to stay at home. He was never happier than when working around the land. The younger son, Lorcan, was a very different kettle of fish. He wasn't interested in land. He felt the call of the ocean and was an adventurer, a rascal with a mischievous sense of humour and a love of money. He owned a galley in which he roamed the wild seas and was involved in acts of piracy and other wealth-making exercises. As a result, he grew rich.

Lorcan was away from home when old Conn became very ill. He sent for Conn.

'Conn, my son,' he said, 'I'm dying. I want to treat you and Lorcan equally. If he was here I would divide my lands into two and give you a half each.

'Lorcan's not here. He's somewhere on the high seas. We haven't seen hilt nor hare of him for some time. He could be dead, for all we know.

'If I divide my land into two and leave half to Lorcan, it would go to waste if he doesn't come back to claim it. If I give all my land to you, will you make a sacred promise to me that you will give Lorcan his fair share if he comes back?'

Secretly, Conn thought that it would be very unfair for Lorcan to inherit half of his father's land. Lorcan was not interested in land and he wouldn't want to take care of it. Conn smiled and said.

'Father I will take Lorcan to a high place, tell him to look around and I will say to him, 'All the land, as far as the eye can see, is yours.'

The old man was satisfied and died in peace.

When Lorcan returned, he was very upset to hear of the death of his father.

Conn the Younger told Lorcan of his promise, taking him up the mountain pass by the Bog of Aenagh and telling him to look around. All the land he could see was his.

Lorcan laughed heartily. In his eyes, land was for people who liked to stay at home and look after it. He was an adventurer at heart; he'd feel trapped if he owned a lot of land. The small patch of land on which they were standing was high up on the mountain pass and completely surrounded by cliffs. It resembled a hole in the ground rather than a vast tract of land, but Lorcan was happy with his inheritance. He enjoyed the joke and set off on his adventures again.

Lorcan's galley was a splendid ship and he started to trade with the East, which wasn't as dangerous an occupation as piracy and much more profitable. While returning to Cadiz from a trading voyage, he saw a Moorish pirate dhow attack a yawl, which looked as if it had set out from Cadiz on a pleasure trip. It was flying the Spanish flag and Lorcan decided he should go to the rescue. He fought the pirates off, put them to flight and escorted the yawl safely back to harbour. There he was invited ashore by the rescued grateful Don and his equally grateful daughter.

The Don gave a banquet in honour of Lorcan and praised his bravery and courage. Unfortunately, Lorcan's mischievous sense of humour got the better of him; he was amused by the extravagant praise heaped upon him and decided to play to the gallery. He boasted, with his tongue in his cheek, that he was the Chieftain of Aneagh: he could stand at a great height on the mountains of his homeland, and all the land as far as he could see belonged to him.

Lorcan fell in love with the Don's daughter, the beautiful Cauthleen, asked her to marry him and promised to spend the rest of his life making her happy. He knew he was very wealthy and could support her in the manner to which she had been accustomed.

Cauthleen was dazzled by Lorcan. She admired his height, his courage, his good looks and, most of all, his tales of wealth, so agreed to his proposal. She was nearly 7ft tall, 3in smaller than Lorcan, who was a veritable Finn McCool. Her father's people were of the Royal Line of Spain while her mother came from the princely O'Donnells, a branch of which had settled in Spain. Her mother was also called Cauthleen, which is how she got her Irish Christian name.

But, when Lorcan asked the Don for Cauthleen's hand, it was refused. The Don explained that Cauthleen was a valuable asset; her hand was much sought after. It was her moral duty to make an alliance that would cement a political agreement, and she was already betrothed to a suitable husband.

Lorcan felt very dejected and when he told Cauthleen of her father's decision she was furious. She was a woman of spirit, and very firmly told her father she did not want to be exchanged in marriage for some sort of political agreement. She wanted to marry Lorcan, to travel with him and to go up the mountain and look at his land where she would have a share in all that she could see.

Lorcan laughed. Love is blind, and he had no idea Cauthleen cared more about his possessions than about him.

The lovers eloped and set sail together, drifting across the sea and enjoying balmy breezes and gentle waves softy lapping on the galley's sides. They felt as if they were in heaven and their marriage was bliss.

Eventually, Lorcan decided it was time to go home. It was a lovely sunny day when the young couple disembarked at Omeath. Cauthleen's face was wreathed in smiles. She was delighted by the beauty of the countryside and laughed with pleasure when she was welcomed by the friendly locals, who were astonished by her appearance. Her hair was powdered with violet dust and gathered up in a tower above her head, making her look even taller than she really was. She wore an expensive Spanish mantle with its rich folds trailing behind her. Her long neck was adorned with strings of precious gems that sparkled like fire in the sunlight. Her beauty was such and she looked so exotic that she will be remembered for all time in Omeath.

Cauthleen declared that she would like to be taken to the high point of Lorcan's land to see what he had described for her.

A gentle breeze wafted the sweet smell of yellow whin blossom through the air. Cauthleen was enchanted as she looked down on Carlingford Lough shimmering like a gem below. The air of the emerald green glens was filled with scent and a translucent blue haze, which made the Mourne Mountains appear like fairyland.

They moved higher and higher up the mountain track. Surely all this beautiful land and more belonged to her wealthy husband, thought Cauthleen.

Cauthleen turned to Lorcan, saying she thought it was a wonderful country in which to live in. She had never felt happier in her whole life and she couldn't wait to see his lands. He told her to be patient, they were very near Aenagh, the land which he loved, which had belonged to his ancestors and which was in his blood.

At last they reached the enclosure in the rocks. Lorcan kissed his bride gently and told her to stand in the centre of the 'Lug' and look around. He laughed as he told her that he was lord of all she could survey.

Cauthleen gazed around in horror. She could see nothing but high rocks enclosing a small space. She was very disappointed and absolutely furious. Lorcan, however, seemed to think it was a joke! As far as she was concerned, it was not funny. He had fooled her. She had given up everything for him – rank, wealth, a suitable marriage, and for what? This hole in the ground? Like most 'long' people, she had a weak heart. The disappointment and rage were too much for her to bear. She uttered a loud gasp, clutched her chest as it was gripped by pain and dropped dead.

Lorcan was horrified at her reaction to what he considered a good joke. He knew he was wealthy. He could afford to give his bride everything she wanted! They should have been able to live happily together. As far as he was concerned, the land was not important. He was an adventurer who loved the sea. He rushed over to Cauthleen.

'Cauthleen! Cauthleen! Wake up! Wake up!' he yelled.

There was no response. She had stopped breathing. He desperately tried to revive her, realised she was dead, became mad with grief and ran up the steep mountain path to where the road forks around the Bog of Aenagh. He was in such despair that he flung himself into the bog and was sucked under its murky waters.

Later that day, people who had watched the galley sail up the lough in the morning and been so pleased to have Lorcan home again and to meet with his beautiful, exotic bride, wondered what had happened to the couple. Why hadn't they returned? Eventually, they began the long walk up the mountain path and found the body of the 'Long Woman' lying in the enclosure of the rocks. There was no sign of Lorcan.

They dug a grave for Cauthleen and buried her where she lay. Each one present threw a stone on her grave to raise her burial cairn and mark the spot. Lorcan's body was never found, but locals still show visitors the 'Cairn of Cauthleen', or 'The Long Woman's Grave', and they still believe that throwing a stone on it ensures a long happy marriage.

14

THE JUMPING CHURCH AT KILDEMOCK

Staff in the tourist information office in St Patrick Centre, Downpatrick, told me about the jumping church near Ardee. I was intrigued and went to see it. If you are interested, you will find it south of Ardee, just off N2. Leave Ardee by Collon Road, turn left and follow the signposts.

The ancient ruined church of Kildemock is surrounded by mystery. Local folklore tells of a strange event that occurred on Candlemas Day 1715: one of the outer walls, which is 19ft high, 15ft wide and built of stones, suddenly jumped approximately 3ft off its foundations and landed, intact, inside the church, albeit at a jaunty angle.

Time passed, and the old churchyard became overgrown. Few people, if any, visited it.

In 1953 Canon Demot McIver, who was the curate in Ardee (1940–60), and Michael O'Flynn obtained a grant from Louth Archaeological Society to restore graveyards in the parish. To everyone's great amazement, they found the old folk tale to be true. When the accumulated debris of centuries was removed, and the true outline of the church's foundations were revealed it could be seen that one of the outer walls of the ancient ruin really was standing erect inside the foundations, as described by the local oral tradition.

Local folklore provides two explanations for this strange phenomenon. Some say it was caused by a freak wind on Candlemas Day 1715. Others say the church was defiled when the body of excommunicated man was buried within its walls. The man concerned was a stonemason, who fell to his death from scaffolding while working on Stabannon church. He had been excommunicated because he had been born to Catholic stock, but had renounced his religious faith and embraced the Protestant religion. After his death, his distraught relatives couldn't find a place to bury him: all the local churches refused permission. In those days, the Catholic Church would have nothing to do with excommunicated members, and people believed that if you were not buried in consecrated ground, you had no chance of going to heaven. That belief must have upset the grieving relatives, who obviously believed that their loved one was a good man and worthy of burial in a Christian graveyard. Nobody knows when it took place; probably secretly late one dark, moonless night well away from clerics, who knew nothing about it.

Kildemock church is part of Ardee parish which, during the Middle Ages, included the townlands of Paughanstown, Roestown, Hacklin, Millockstown, Hunterstown, Anaglog, Rathlust, Kilpatrick, Drakestown and Blakestown. The name 'Kilpatrick' is particularly interesting, because the word '*kil*' or '*cil*' means old church. Patrick is Ireland's patron saint, so the name suggests that the church was founded by St Patrick himself. The churchyard is obviously very ancient because it contains numerous tiny headstones, dating back to Celtic times.

Kildemock church was once called Millockstown church. It is said to have been founded by St Diomac, an early disciple of St Patrick. In the early days of Christianity in Ireland, St Patrick chose one of his followers – Diomoc, also known as Modiomoc – to bring Christianity to the parish, so there is a tenuous connection between Ireland's patron saint and the jumping church.

After the Norman invasion during the twelfth century, the parish came under control of the Knights Templar, lineal ancestors of the Knights of Malta. In 1313, the church was dedicated to St Catherine. Who would have thought that the jumping church in a sleepy parish south of Ardee, surrounded by a peaceful grave-yard with a spectacular views of the Carlingford and Mourne Mountains would have such exotic foreign connections?

Sadly, Kildemock church fell into ruins when King Henry VIII destroyed all religious houses refusing to recognise him as head of the church.

15

ORIGIN OF THE RIVER BOYNE

I got this story from Michael Scott who tells a good yarn and writes beautifully.

The River Boyne arises gradually from bogs and marshes at the foot of a hill the ancients called '*Sidh Nechtain*'. It runs for a short distance between County Kildare and County Offaly before running into County Meath. It continues in a north-easterly direction past Clonard, Trim and Navan before sweeping past the ancient burial tombs in the Boyne Valley and on to Oldbridge in County Louth before flowing through Drogheda and into the Irish Sea at Invra Colpa, which is between Mornington and Baltray.

Boann was 16 years of age, very beautiful, spoilt and headstrong when she was forced to marry Nectain. She didn't like him much. He was old and grizzled and not much fun. She was bored. He kept leaving her, going out on his own and telling her she couldn't come.

'Why can't I come?' she kept asking petulantly. 'Why do I have to stay at home while you go out enjoying yourself? I'm bored, do you understand? BORED!'

'Be reasonable,' said Nectain, trying to be patient. He found his young wife, with her constant demands, a bit of a pain. He had married her for political reasons and was disappointed in her.

He had hoped his young wife would have been a help, but all she did was complain. He was fed up with her demands and her vanity and pride.

'Boann, I've told you before, you simply can't come. You know my family were chosen to guard the magic well. The Tuatha De Danann blessed its waters with their magical powers for the use of the people of Erin. Sadly, powerful chieftains and kings became greedy and grew rich by charging for use of the waters. The result was terrible. The people rose up in revolt and the druids took the situation into their own hands. They decided one honourable family should care for the well and its magical waters; misuse had caused its water level to sink dangerously low so it could only be used during times of plague. My family were proud and delighted to be chosen. We are the only people allowed near it. Looking after the well is a very responsible job. What I have to do is serious and dangerous.'

'Why can't I be treated with the respect I deserve? After all, I'm married to you so I'm a member of your family. I should be allowed to visit the well,' Boann complained.

'That's true, to a certain extent, but your blood is different from my blood. It would be very dangerous for you to go anywhere near the well. Our children will carry my blood and be able to go. You can't and that's that.'

'So I'm to be used as breeding stock to provide keepers for that stupid old well? My children will be able to go into places where I'm not allowed to venture. That's unfair and stupid,' Boann snapped. 'Everyone knows the well is just a hole in the ground sur-rounded by smoothly rounded stones somewhere in the middle of the forest. You're making a fuss over nothing.'

'That's not true. The well isn't just a simple hole. A crystal wall was built around it in the past and an ornate wooden cover overlaid with gold placed on top of it to keep a single drop of the precious water escaping.'

'Now stop girning. You know my brothers and I have to make obeisance to the well at full moon. Content yourself and get on with your spinning.'

Boann was furious, but felt it wise to hide her feelings. She smiled, sat down by the roaring fire in the great hall and started spinning.

'Woman's work,' she thought. 'I hate woman's work. I'm as good as any man. Why should I sit here meekly spinning while my so-called lord and master swans off into the forest? I'll find out where he's going. I'll follow him. I'll visit the well.'

Boann had studied enough magical lore to know that magicians visiting ancient places of power have to be spotlessly clean. Bad spirits and malignant influences are attracted by dirt and can attach themselves to it. She watched sourly as Nectain purified himself, removing all metals, washing in the spring running beside his fort and changing his clothing.

When Nectain came to say goodbye, Boann lowered her head modestly so her ash blond hair shone in the firelight.

'Huh,' she muttered, 'I bet there's not much magic left in the well anyway. I bet it's just a useless pool of water.'

'That's not true,' Nectain replied. 'My family have guarded the precious waters of the well for many generations. They have not been misused. Now the magic is stronger than ever.'

Boann waited patiently until Nectain and his brothers had left, then followed them through the ancient forest. She realised leaving the track would be dangerous at night, because she might trip over an exposed root, fall and break a leg. She followed the track carefully, deep into the heart of the wood, and was disappointed when she came out the other side. Nectain and his brothers must have turned off somewhere, but where? She decided she had no chance of finding the well by herself and the best thing she could do was to get back to the fort before her husband returned. But she felt more determined than ever. She was not going to be beaten. She would visit the forbidden well, but she must find out more about it. She kept questioning her husband and he enraged her by refusing to answer.

'I've heard that anyone drinking the well's magic water will live forever. Have you ever drunk from it?'

'Why would I want to do that? I've seen all I want to see, done all I want to do. Now I'm just looking forward to being released from this life's troubles. I look forward to entering the Otherworld.

I'm 40 years of age, old, gnarled and ancient. I've had enough of this world and I'll be glad to leave.'

'How can you say you have had enough? You haven't done anything but guard that stupid old well. You've never even left the valley. Have you never longed for adventure? To see more of life? To have fun?'

Nectain shook his head. 'No, I think they're foolish notions. You should be content with what you've got and make the best of it. It's silly to go looking for greener fields.'

'Well, I think you're an old stick in the mud. I want adventure. I'm bored here in this backwood of a forest. I can see nothing but trees, trees, trees and more trees. I can hear nothing but the rustle of leaves. I want life, laughter, music. I want to dance, sing, have fun. Please take me to the well.'

Boann got up and danced around the room. Nectain sighed. He should never have married her. She would never be content; she would always search for an impossible dream.

She grabbed his wizened hand. 'Please, please, please take me to the well.'

'I can't. It's forbidden. I've told you, the well must be treated with respect. It's dangerous.'

'But I would treat it with respect.'

'You're a woman. Women mustn't go near the well. Only men from my family are allowed to approach it.'

Boann was determined to follow her husband and his brothers when they next visited the well. When the time came, she donned a long dark cloak and slid silently into the darkness behind them. She knew they would suddenly disappear off the familiar track, so watched carefully. They didn't notice the shadow behind them. Clan Nectain moved silently through the ancient forest, while Boann kept as close to the group as she dared. She noted carefully where the men put their feet.

'There're bound to be booby traps along the way,' she thought. 'That's what Nectain means when he says it's dangerous.'

At one point, the men took an extra long step over a gnarled root. She followed and shivered as she glanced down. What she thought was a root was in fact a spiked bar. At another point the men left the path. Boann followed but looked carefully to see if she could find out why they had avoided that particular place. It was a pit hidden under a covering of leaves and grass.

It was almost midnight when Clan Nectain reached the magic well. Boann watched from a distance, feeling very disappointed. She had thought the well would be beautiful, with shining crystal walls and a lovely golden covering. It looked very ordinary. The crystal walls looked dirty and the gold skin covering the wooden cover was shabby, peeling off in places and covered in moss. She watched as her husband and his brothers moved around the pool. They were obviously carrying out some ancient ritual.

'Mumbo jumbo,' she thought, 'I thought Nectain had more sense than to believe in that kind of rubbish. There's nothing to that silly old well. It's much ado about nothing. It's not dangerous. It's just an old useless ruin, like my husband.'

The men ended the ceremony by lowering a polished wooden cup into the depths of the well. Each brother drew out a cupful of water and ceremoniously poured it on the ground. There was a flash of light. The brothers bowed towards the well, backed out of the clearing and vanished down the path.

Boann kept hidden behind the trees until they had disappeared from sight, then walked firmly up to the well, looked at it and walked three times in an anti-clockwise direction round it.

'Have Nectain and his brothers spent their entire lives watching this boring old well?' she thought. 'They're fools. Absolute fools.'

She stopped and ran her hand over the golden cover. Mosses and lichens were growing on it, hiding the ancient complicated pattern. She ran her hand over the design, tracing loops, curves and spirals. The sixteen stones circling the clearing behind her suddenly sprang to life and began to sparkle and glitter as they burned with white fire. Boann had her back to them and didn't see what they were doing. She roughly shoved back the well's cover and gazed down into its murky depths.

'Huh,' she muttered, 'I can't see anything there. It's a dead loss. I wonder what the water tastes like? Would it make me live forever? It's worth a try.'

She took the wooden cup and lowered it down, down and down into the depths of the well. Eventually she heard a splash as the cup reached the waters and she began to pull it up again. It was very heavy; surprisingly heavy for such a small cup. Her arms and shoulders became sore with the effort of pulling and pulling and she was out of breath by the time it reached the top. She breathed a sigh of relief and took a sip. The water was like nothing she had ever tasted. It was icy cold and oily. It hit the back of her throat and burnt its way down her gullet like the strongest mead. She liked it and drank the whole cupful.

'The men were crazy throwing this on the ground,' she thought. 'This is great stuff.'

She threw back her head and laughed as the effects hit her. She was no longer exhausted. She felt the magic water rushing through her body, making it strong, warm and impervious to the chill air of night.

'That really was *uisce bestha*, the breath of life!' she shouted in triumph.

The sixteen standing stones that had been set to guard the sacred well lumbered into life. Each was as tall and as wide as a man. They were monsters, and they lumbered noisily towards Boann. She whirled around at the sound and screamed. The stones then formed a circular wall around her and closed in on her, forcing her into the well. She screamed as she fell. The crystal walls caught her scream and sent it out into the forest as a terrified wail. Leaves trembled on branches, ancient timbers groaned and rasped, and the very forest shook. The well exploded and the crystal rocks and standing stones shattered and tumbled as a column of silver water erupted, knocking out Boann's eye and disfiguring her face before slicing through the forest towards the ocean. It left a trail of devastation in its path, swallowing men, animals, and whole communities on its mad journey to the sea. Those who were awake at the time caught a glimpse of a wild-haired woman in the column of water, which was christened the River Boyne.

There's still magic in the water. If you sit quietly by the River Boyne and drink in its beauty, you may feel its healing power.

16

MAIDEN TOWER
AT MORNINGTON

Brendan Matthews, historian at the Drogheda Museum at Millmount, Drogheda, gave me this story.

She was beautiful and he felt very tempted to do what she wanted when she pleaded with him.

'Please, darling, don't leave me. Don't go to war. Fighting's dangerous. You could be killed. I love you so much, I couldn't bear to live without you. I couldn't even bear to see your ship on the horizon and wonder if you were dead or alive.'

The young man was in love and she was very pretty. Then he remembered. All his friends were going to war. He had to join them. It would be dishonourable to stay behind. He became adamant.

'Darling, I don't want to leave you. I hate the idea of going into battle. But I'll be branded as a coward if I stay behind. I'll ask the captain to fly a black flag if I'm dead, and a white one if I'm alive, so you'll know what's happened the moment you see my ship.'

The maiden went to live alone in Maiden Tower at Mornington. It's an Elizabethan tower house built towards the end of the sixteenth century, during the reign of Queen Elizabeth I, and said to be named in honour of the 'Maiden Queen' herself. It's a square building, which stands at a height of over 35ft. There are battlements at the top and the parapet is reached through a barrel-vault at the end of the spiral staircase. For centuries it's been a conspicuous landmark, guiding seafarers safely towards the estuary of the River Boyne and the port of Drogheda.

For weeks on end the young maiden kept watch over the sea, her eyes eagerly seeking her lover's ship. At last she spotted it, and what did she see? The dreaded black flag. She was distraught; she could not live without her lover. She climbed up to the parapet, jumped off the tower and was killed. Another tower, known as The Needle, was built to mark the spot where her broken body landed. It's much thinner than Maiden Tower and built of solid stone, topped by a simple cone-shaped structure, resembling the top many farmers put on gate posts to keep the fairies from sitting on them.

Maiden Tower lay empty for years because it was believed to be unlucky. Then, one brisk March morning in 1819, some local fisherman who were at the Boyne's estuary saw smoke coming out of the chimney. They wondered what was going on. Who had built the fire? Had anyone gone to live there? They decided to investigate, entered the building, climbed the fifty-five steep steps to the top and were amazed to see a fire burning brightly in the grate. There was a neat pile of dry marron grass covered with a quilt in the corner. An ancient woman with silver hair and a wrinkled face was sitting on a small wooden stool in the corner, spinning thread.

'Where have you come from?' asked the inquisitive fishermen.

'I lived in Drogheda when I was a child, a long, long time ago, before I went on my travels. I had a vision telling me to come back to my hometown and to end my days in peace here. I don't want to be asked any more questions. I can't be bothered giving endless explanations. I'm perfectly alright, and I'm not doing anyone any harm. I just want to be left alone. I'm happy here. As you can see, I can collect driftwood for my fire and marron grass makes a very comfortable bed. I sleep on that pile in the corner. I don't need anything more.'

The old lady refused to tell anyone her name. She lived in the tower for approximately two years, becoming a familiar sight in the neighbourhood. She appeared to have a strange knowledge of ancient tales and herbal remedies and spent her days working hard at her spinning wheel. Every week, she gave the items she had spun to the church at Mornington to be sold to help the poor.

The winter of 1821 was very harsh. The old lady felt the cold terribly and her health declined rapidly. She went into the charity house in Fair Street, Drogheda, where she died and was buried in Cord cemetery. Yet she remained a complete mystery. Who was she? Where had she come from? She said she had spent her childhood in Drogheda, yet nobody recognised her. Why? Was she real? Was she a spirit in a human body? Did that spirit belong to the tragic maiden who had jumped from the tower so many years ago? Had she come back to the neighbourhood to make amends for taking her own life? Nobody knows.

17

THE SALMON OF
KNOWLEDGE

This was one of Granny Henry's stories. She used to laugh when she told me what happened. 'Poor auld Finn Eces,' she said, 'he was mightily disappointed but sure, didn't he take it in good heart. It's not what happens to you in life that matters, it's how you react to it. Finn Eces did the right thing. He accepted the inevitable and helped his young servant become one of the greatest leaders of all time. He has gone down in history. His name is remembered, just not in the way he wanted. He aimed at the stars and hit the moon, but sure, that's better than remaining on the ground aiming at nothing.'

A hazel tree was the first thing to come into creation and its branches contained all the knowledge of the universe. It grew over the Well of Wisdom (*Tobar Segais*) and its nuts dropped one by one into the well. A great speckled salmon lived in the well and ate nine of the hazel nuts. As a result, knowledge of the universe was absorbed into its body.

Eventually, the Well of Wisdom was absorbed into the River Boyne, where it formed a deep pool. The great speckled salmon lived there undisturbed for many years. Its fame spread throughout the land and it was said that whosoever ate the flesh of the salmon would possess knowledge of the universe. It was foretold that the first person to taste the flesh of the salmon would be a man called Finn.

Finn Eces was a great poet. 'I am called Finn,' he thought, 'I should seek the Salmon of Knowledge. Just think of how more knowledge would improve my poetry! I could become the greatest poet of all time. My name would go down in history and I would never be forgotten.'

He was filled with ambition and set out to catch the great salmon, but the fish was wily. It refused to take the bait. Finn Eces was a patient man. He visited the pool every day for seven years and fished and fished and fished. Eventually his patience was rewarded and he caught the salmon. He was delighted.

Finn Eces had a servant, a young lad called Finn McCool. He gave the salmon to young Finn and said, 'Light a fire and cook this fine fish very carefully. Don't burn it and whatever you do, you mustn't eat any of its flesh. Do you understand?'

'Yes, master. I will do as you say.'

The young lad was very eager to please his master. He prepared a fire, placed the salmon on a spit and watched it carefully, turning the spit regularly so the salmon would be evenly cooked. The salmon was almost ready when he burnt his thumb as he turned the spit. Young Finn jumped back and instinctively eased the pain by sucking the burn.

When the salmon was cooked, Finn McCool told his master, who came and looked at him. Finn McCool's eyes appeared entirely different. They sparkled with knowledge. A great fear entered Finn Eces heart. Had the boy eaten the salmon? Perhaps he had wasted his time. Perhaps he should have concentrated on writing poetry for the past seven years and not gone fishing.

'Did you eat the salmon?' he asked.

'No, master. You told me not eat the salmon. I didn't touch it.'

'Well, something's happened. Your eyes look different. Tell me about cooking the fish.'

'Please master, I did everything you asked. I made a spit and skewered the fish on it, suspended it over the fire, watched it very carefully and turned it regularly.'

'And you didn't put any of the fish into your mouth? You didn't even have a wee taste, did you?'

'No, sir. I didn't have a wee taste. You can see, the salmon is complete. I didn't touch it.'

'Did you put anything into your mouth?'

'Please sir, I burnt my thumb and sucked it. Look. My thumb's all red. It's still sore.'

Finn Ecles examined his servant's thumb.

'That explains it,' he said. 'You're a good boy. It wasn't your fault. Some of the salmon's substance must have splashed on to your thumb and you swallowed it when you sucked it. Come on lad, the fates are against me. You might as well eat the rest of the salmon.

With the knowledge he gained from the salmon the young Finn McCool was able to become one of the greatest leaders of all time, the leader of the Fianna.

Finn Eces quickly got over his disappointment, concentrating on writing poetry and took great pride in his servant's deeds.

18

THE HAUNTED HOUSE
NEAR DROGHEDA

This is another one of the stories given to me by Brendan
Matthews, historian at the Drogheda Museum at Millmount,
Drogheda, County Louth. He found this horrific story in an old
manuscript.

'Hahaha!' laughed the tailor, 'Pull the other leg. It's got bells on it.
Do you think I'm not the full shillin'? Thon's a crazy yarn you're
telling me. Ghosts indeed! Stuff and nonsense. Thon's a perfectly
good house, so it is. I'm more than happy to go and live in it. It's
a nice size, the rooms are beautiful. I don't believe in ghosts, so I'll
rent the house without further ado. I think some people have too
much imagination. Whoever heard of devils from the lower world
coming to live in a house near Drogheda. They've better things
to do. Horrible noises and awful things seen by perfectly sane
people who went and lived in it. Hahaha! Ballacks! That's a load
of rubbish. People who talk like that are half a sandwich short of a
picnic, that's what. Huh! I repeat, stuff and nonsense. Ghosts! I've
never heard of such a load of auld codswallop in all my life.'

The tailor insisted on renting the house in spite of all the advice
given. He promptly moved in with his wife, their children and the
children's nurse. At first they were very happy. They loved their new

home: it had plenty of space and everything was fine – until the ghost appeared one night, about a week later. The tailor and his wife were going to bed and were putting their nightclothes on when their bedroom door burst open. A twisted clubfoot of somebody they couldn't see kicked the candlestick off the table, leaving them in total darkness. They screamed in terror and stood shivering with shock and fear, when the room suddenly became bright. It appeared as it did in daylight, although it was a very dark, moonless night, and the shutters were closed across the windows and didn't let any light in. Suddenly, a woman came into the room. She was dressed in white and carrying something in her hand, which she threw at the tailor's wife, who staggered at the force of the blow. The woman in white disappeared as quickly as she had appeared.

There was a terrible commotion overhead. The couple were horrified to hear their children screaming.

'The children! The children!' gasped the tailor's wife. 'Something awful's happening to our children! Quick!'

The tailor dashed up stairs into the children's nursery. He was aghast. His poor children were lying on their beds, having been stripped naked and beaten unconscious. Their furniture was trashed. The floor had been torn up, making it difficult to walk across the room, so he had to balance on the rafters. He picked his children up and was about to carry them downstairs, when he realised that he hadn't seen their nurse. He retraced his steps but couldn't find her anywhere. Later he discovered that the terrified girl had been badly beaten up and was covered in bruises. She had fled to her mother's house, where she sadly died a few days later.

The next morning, the tailor's family left the haunted house for good. From that day until the day he died, the tailor no longer scoffed at the idea of ghosts.

19

SAINT OLIVER PLUNKETT (1625–1681)

I became interested in St Oliver Plunkett when I read that a five o'clock shadow can be clearly seen on his embalmed head in Saint Peter's Church Drogheda, proving that he shaved on the morning of his execution. What kind of man would shave before being beheaded for treason.

I visited St Oliver Plunket's head in Drogheda and found its serene expression astonishing. His blackened face does not look as if it belongs to a person who had suffered a violent death. A half smile on his lips reveals beautiful teeth. Local historian Paddy Rispin, from Trim, told me that workers in the seventeenth century had blackened, rotting teeth by the time they were 20 and their life expectation was low. The ruling classes kept their teeth until they were about 30 years old, while the clergy had healthy lifestyles and retained their teeth until they were in their late sixties or early seventies. St Oliver Plunkett was a cleric, which explains his beautiful teeth.

Father Quinn, parish priest of Louth Village, very kindly took me to the ruined church at Ardpatrick and to St Patrick's Well, which is in a field on the road from Louth village to Inniskeen.

Oliver Plunkett was born at Loughcrew, County Meath, near the border with Louth, where his father, John Plunkett, owned a small estate until it was confiscated by Oliver Cromwell during the 1641 rebellion, when the whole of Ireland was ablaze. At that time, Ulster Presbyterians and Catholics united in an attempt to overthrow the English government. Cromwell's troops devastated Ireland, indiscriminately killing men, women and children, laying waste to the land, destroying buildings, animals and crops and causing a famine, the likes of which had never been seen before. The young Oliver Plunkett's family realised his life was in danger and sent him to continue his education in Rome.

Oliver grew to be tall and erect, and his handsome face was framed by a well-trimmed beard and a shoulder-length wig. His eyes were compassionate and penetrating. He was a complex character, capable of inspiring consuming hate and undying love. He could be touchy and hot tempered, but he had a passion for peace and civilised living. He inherited his family's pride, took great care in his appearance and placed great store on nobility of birth.

The decade of war in the 1640s was followed by a decade of persecutions in the 1650s of those who did not belong to the Established Anglican Church, namely native Irish Catholics and Ulster Presbyterians. They were denied education and could be severely punished for not attending Anglican church services. Irish people have a great love of learning, which can be traced back to the ancient Celts. In response, the Irish Catholics and Ulster Presbyterians organised Hedge Schools, which educated children in secret places: behind hedges, in the bogs or secretly in dwellings. To be found by the authorities teaching in, or attending a hedge school or a church service, apart from one organised by the established church was punishable by law. Thousands of people were taken to Dublin, sent for trial and sentenced to be hanged, drawn and quartered, burnt at the stake or transported as a slave to the New World.

Oliver returned to Ireland in 1670 as Bishop of Armagh, the head of the Roman Catholic Church in Ireland. In the summer of 1671 he moved into a residence with the Jesuit Fathers near

Dundalk. He knew his life was in danger, so during his first few months as Primate disguised himself as 'Captain Browne' by wearing a wig and pistols and a sword, allaying suspicions by singing in taverns and kissing the ladies.

Oliver was horrified when he saw what had happened to education in Ireland. He believed that knowledge was power, so one of his first acts as archbishop was to set up several schools, probably near Dundalk in the region of Ballybarrack. He provided everything his schools needed, 'even the frying pan', and spent more on supplying them with materials than he earned as Archbishop of Armagh.

Eventually the Catholic Church in Rome gave him a little financial help (150 *scudi*, which is about £37.50 a year). His schools expanded, so he moved them to Drogheda in 1672. He reckoned that was the best place for them because the Jesuits had a fine chapel there and Drogheda was by far the largest town in the archdiocese during the seventeenth century.

Oliver lived as economically as possible, dressing poorly and eating cheap food so he could subsidise his schools and keep them open. At their height, he was providing education for twenty-five ecclesiastics and 150 boys, forty of whom were Presbyterians. The schools lasted three years before being levelled by the authorities in 1673 and Oliver was forced into hiding. He was so upset by the destruction of his schools that years later he wrote: 'There is nothing that occasions me more inward grief than to see the schools instituted by me now destroyed after so many toils. Oh what will youth do, which is both numerous and full of talent?'

Local folklore states that Ardpatrick church was founded by St Patrick himself and that two of the saint's surviving letters were found there: his 'Confession' and the 'Letter to Coroticus'.

The church is approached by a grass path leading through several fields. It is situated near the top of a hill and is very well hidden by a high hedge on one side and by being sunk into the hillside on the other. There is a beautiful view of the countryside from the top of the hill, which allowed lookouts to see, and warn, of approaching soldiers looking for illegal church services or education classes.

Local tradition refers to the site of Oliver's house, near which is near the garden wall of Ardpatrick House. There is an ancient oak tree nearby which is still called 'Blessed Oliver's Bed' and 'Blessed Oliver's Oak'. It is said he used to hide there when government forces were seeking to arrest him.

Castletown Castle and Louth Hall are also associated with St Oliver Plunkett and there is a strong tradition that sometimes he hid in the Mullabawn Valley under the shadow of Slieve Gullion.

Louth Hall belonged to Lord Louth, who was Oliver's cousin. Oliver had use of a secluded room and often hid in the icehouse, which was surrounded by a dense thicket of laurels. Information about Oliver's visits to his cousin has been passed down in an unbroken line from a succession of gardeners working in Louth Hall. Oliver's first period 'on the run' lasted until 1675. Judging from his letters, it was a miserable existence. He wrote during December 1673:

> I am hiding and Dr Brennan is with me ... I sometimes find it hard to even get oaten bread, and the house where Dr Brennan and I are staying is made of straw and covered or thatched so badly that we can see the stars when we are in bed, and even the slightest shower of rain sprinkles our pillows. But we are determined to die of hunger and cold rather than desert our flocks ...

On 27 January 1674, he wrote:

> There was a biting north wind blowing into our faces and it beat the snow and hail so fiercely into our eyes that even now we can scarcely see with them. Many times we were in danger of being lost in the valleys and of dying of suffocation in the snow ... The cold and the hail were so terrible that my eyes have not yet stopped running nor have those of my companion. I feel that I shall lose more than one tooth, they are paining me so much, and my companion was attacked with rheumatism in one arm and can scarcely move it ...

Many places are associated with Oliver as hiding places, including caves at Killeavy and Faughart, the cairn on the top of Slieve Gullion and the Cadgers' Pass, which is a mountain pass leading from Omeath to Ravensdale.

Oliver rode from place to place on horseback, apart from a few visits to Dublin when he travelled by mail coach. He kept at least one stable boy and a servant, James McKenna. In 1679 he heard that his old teacher, the Bishop of Meath, was on his deathbed, and went to visit his old friend one last time. He disguised himself by cutting his beard and hair off and putting on a light-coloured wig. Thus disguised as 'Mr Meleady', he set out for Dublin. What Oliver didn't know was that he, along with Colonel John Fitzpatrick and two bishops, were suspected of plotting to bring a French army to Ireland and a warrant had been issued for his arrest.

Sir Hans Hamilton of Hamiltonsbawn, near Armagh, was given the job of catching Oliver. Sir Hans was a wily man. He told the local parish priest he needed to communicate urgently with Oliver, so the priest innocently told him that Oliver was staying near The Naul and gave details of his disguise. As a result, Oliver was arrested in Dublin on 6 December and locked up in Dublin Castle. He was kept in solitary confinement and nobody was allowed to visit him, not even his servant. Trumped up 'evidence' was fabricated by clerics and others, which caused Oliver to end up in Newgate Prison in London. He was kept in irons in solitary confinement and had to pay for his room and food, and even his shackles. When his money ran out, he petitioned 'to be maintained upon His Majesty's charge'. The petition was granted and the keeper was allowed 10s a week to support him. His servant, James McKenna, brought him a change of linen and was locked up in a nearby cell for his pains.

Several attempts were made to get the grand jury to condemn Oliver, but these failed, because witnesses for the prosecution were unreliable and there was no evidence against him. His enemies in the Catholic Church decided to coach witnesses before their next appeared in court, to ensure that they gave the 'right' answers. As a result, Oliver was condemned and sentenced to death by hanging.

Things became easier for Oliver once he had been sentenced. He was allowed to see his servant. He seemed happy and spent most of his time praying. He slept soundly the night before he died and said Mass when he awoke. The governor of Newgate Prison reported:

> When I came to him this morning he was newly awake, having slept all night without any disturbance; and when I told him to prepare for his execution, he received the message with all quietness of mind, and went to the sledge as if he was going to a wedding.

Tyburn was about two miles from Newgate and the journey must have taken roughly an hour, as the streets were paved with cobblestones and thronged with people. The gallows were situated in what is now the middle of the street at Hyde Park Corner. They were wide, so it was possible to hang twenty people at once. Bodies were usually left on the gallows until they turned black, as a warning to others.

Oliver showed no signs of fear as he mounted the gallows and proceeded to give his 'speech from the gallows'. He said he forgave all those who had played a part in his death. He prayed for the king, queen, Duke of York and the Royal Family. He asked pardon of all those he had offended and prayed for forgiveness of his own sins. His final acts were to recite the psalm *Miserere* and, as the hangman put the noose around his neck and the cap over his eyes, he continued to repeat, 'Into thy hands, O Lord, I commend my spirit,' until the horse had pulled the cart from under his feet and he was left dangling by the neck. At least three priests were near the gallows to give him absolution.

Oliver wrote a long list of English people who had helped him when he was in prison. They included a Mr Sheldon and his family. Elizabeth, Mr Sheldon's wife, was present at the execution, and she obtained the king's permission to receive Oliver's remains. With the help of James McKenna and the three priests, she had the remains brought from the gallows and a Catholic surgeon, John Ridley, removed the two arms at the elbows. The arms were put in a long tin box and the head in a round tin one. Elizabeth Sheldon took care of them and a documentation of authentication was signed by her and by John Ridley on 29 May 1682. The remainder of his body was buried in the churchyard at St Giles-in-the-Fields in London. Eventually it was dug up and placed in a special shrine in the abbey church of Lamspringe in West Germany. In 1883, the remains were again moved to Downside Abbey in England. Since then relics and souvenirs of Oliver have been distributed widely and the door from Newgate Prison through which he walked on his way to execution was removed and is now in St Peter's church, Drogheda.

20

WILLY JOHN'S BIG SURPRISE

My old friend Ernie Scott from Ballynure, County Antrim, first told me this story approximately twenty-five years ago. He told it with reference to Ballynure. Years later, Roisin Cox told me the same story in connection with Carlingford, County Louth. Since then I have received adaptations of the same story by email. It is a story that travels well. Enjoy.

Sister Anne and Sister Petronella belonged to the Sacred Heart Convent, Newry, and they were very pleased with themselves. Sister Anne had learnt to drive and her brother had lent her his brand new wee Austin 7 car. She rushed – as fast as a nun can rush when she's wearing a long black habit on a warm June day – to her friend, Sister Petronella, and asked her if she would like to go for a day out. The Mother Superior had given permission.

Sister Petronella was delighted at the idea and the pair drove out of the convent, turned left past the old Victoria Bakery (now Bagnel's Castle Museum), across the bridge over the River Clanryne, along the Newry Canal, past Victoria Docks and along the road towards Carlingford.

Sister Petronella, who was a bit of a philosopher, turned to Sister Anne and said, 'Sure isn't it a beautiful day, and aren't we the lucky nuns to be given a day off and to have been born at a time when we can enjoy modern conveniences such as this grand wee car? If we'd arrived in this world twenty years earlier, we'd have been worried by the Great War, and only the gentry had cars. Now, thanks to Henry Ford, even nuns can go out for a drive. Isn't the life of a nun in the year 1934 absolutely great? And may the Good Lord heap blessings on the head of Henry Ford and his inventions!'

The nuns were about a mile from Carlingford when the car went 'putt, putt, putt … putt … putt …' and stopped. Sister Anne looked with consternation at the petrol gauge. They had run out of juice.

They got out and tried to push the car along the road. It was a hot day, the car was solid and pushing was hard work. Their long black habits hindered them and they began to sweat and become breathless.

'Oh dear, oh dear,' gasped Sister Anne, 'this is going to be the death of me. At this rate of going we'll not reach Carlingford until the middle of next week.'

'Sure,' replied Sister Petronella, 'sure, the Good Lord's been kind to us. Haven't we run out of petrol only a mile or so from our destination? I know this road well. Sure we can easily walk into Carlingford and buy petrol in the spirit grocers. It belongs to Mr O'Hare and he's the quare decent big man. I'm sure he'll find some way to help us.

They picked up their long habits and began to walk towards Carlingford. It was lunchtime when they arrived and the O'Hare's shop appeared empty.

'Yoohoo!' shouted Sister Petronella, 'Yoohoo! Yoohoo!'

'Coming,' shouted a voice from the back of the shop.

A few minutes later P.J. entered. 'Good morning, or should I say good afternoon, sisters. I was having a wee bite to eat – it's lunchtime. But never mind that. What can I do for you?'

Sister Petronella explained the problem.

P.J. said, 'You're right, ladies. I can help. I do sell petrol although to be sure, to be sure, I can't leave the shop at the moment. As I said, it's lunchtime. I'm to keep an eye on the place as there's nobody else here at present.'

'What'll we do?' asked the nuns.

'Your wee car stopped about a mile up the road, didn't it? You must be exhausted, walking in those long robes in the sun. Have you enough energy to get back to the car?'

The nuns agreed they could walk back to the car.

'Tell you what, why don't I give you a wee container with some petrol in it, just enough to get you going again. If I lent you a funnel, you could walk back to the car, screw the cap leading to the petrol tank open, put the funnel into the pipe and pour petrol down the funnel. That should get you going so you can drive back here and I'll fill you up. How about that? Is it a plan?'

The nuns agreed that was a good idea and P.J. looked around the shop for a suitable container. He'd sold the last one of his jugs earlier in the day and the new order hadn't arrived. The only thing he could find was what was known in those days as a 'goes-under', meaning a chamber pot that goes under the bed for use if the occupant is caught short during the night.

P.J. asked the nuns if they minded carrying a 'goes-under' filled with petrol up the road. They laughed and laughed at the idea but agreed, so Sister Anne lifted the large funnel while Sister Petronella carried the 'goes-under' and they left P.J. O'Hare's shop laughing their legs off.

Before long, they reached the Austin 7, where Sister Anne managed to unscrew the petrol cap and inserted the funnel into the pipe. Sister Petronella began to pour petrol carefully into the funnel when along the road came Big Willy John in his pony and trap. Big Willy was a well-known Protestant and a member of the Loyal Orange Order to boot. He saw what the two nuns were doing, stopped in astonishment, climbed down off the cart and went over to take a closer look.

Willy John pushed his old duncher (cap) to the back on his head and scratched behind his ear.

'Ladies,' he said, 'I've got to admit I'm of a different religious persuasion to yourselves but I've got to say, I don't half admire your faith.'

21

THE BLACK DEATH
VISITS LOUTH

Thanks are due to Sean Collins, who not only told me this sad story but took me to see the cadaver tombs in the churchyard of St Peter's Anglican church in Drogheda.

Folklore describes medieval times as being very jolly. We talk about Merrie Olde England. But – and it's a big but – the motto 'Eat, drink and be merry for tomorrow we die' shows that the outer merriment hid a dark secret. People could catch bubonic plague and die very quickly. What happened in England also occurred in Ireland. The general attitude was 'Life is very fragile. We could die within a few days, so we might as well enjoy ourselves while we can', and County Louth was no exception. It suffered from the effects of bubonic plague in the fourteenth century. There is a monument of that time on in the boundary wall of St Peter's Anglican church in Drogheda in the form of two cadaver tombstones. Originally they would have been in a horizontal rather than a vertical position and nobody knows who moved them and placed them up the wall, or why that was done.

Cadaver tombs are gigantic structures, and they are very rare. The ones in St Peter's churchyard are on the east wall, behind the present church. They stretch from the base of the wall up to the top and depict the occupants of the graves with bodies partially enclosed in shrouds. These medieval structures are intended to depict the fragility of life.

The cadaver tombs in St Peter's once covered the bodies of Edward Goldying and his wife Elizabeth Fleming, who died during the plague epidemic that swept Europe, including Ireland, between 1348 and 1350. In medieval times people had no idea of human anatomy, so Edward Goldying appears to have about sixty pairs of ribs. His wife has a hollow abdomen because it was thought that women had a space inside in which to grow babies.

Elizabeth died from the bubonic plague before her husband. He appears to have recovered quickly from his loss because he had three more wives before contracting a fatal strain of plague himself. The extraordinary thing is that Edward only lived for three months after Elizabeth's death. There are those who would say that having three wives in three months would be enough to kill any man!

Smaller memorials commemorating the other three wives are to be found beside the cadaver tombs. They are a grim memorial of a grim period of history.

22

THE BATTLE OF THE BOYNE

Thanks are due to local historian Sean Collins, who told me the story of the Battle of the Boyne in such a way that, for the first time, I really understood what it was all about.

In Ireland, the majority of the population think the Battle of the Boyne was a sectarian confrontation between the Catholic King James II and the Protestant King William III: in other words, a fight between a Catholic and a Protestant. Nothing could be further from the truth. The Battle of the Boyne was a struggle over kingship. Information about the Battle of the Boyne has been distorted by politicians for their own ends for centuries, so the truth has been almost completely lost.

James's daughter, Mary, was married to her father's nephew, William, Prince of Orange. He was from Holland, a staunch Protestant and a very ambitious young man. When the British parliament became dissatisfied with their monarch and began looking for a replacement, William appeared to be the most likely candidate. He was more than willing to apply for the job.

James's cousin, King Louis IVX of France, was another ambitious man. He wanted to expand his territories and rule over the whole of Europe, so began invading European countries. The Pope did not approve and backed the Protestant pretender, William of Orange. William gained the British throne in what became known as 'The Glorious Revolution', because not a single shot was fired nor a single person killed. When Louis heard James had been deposed, he was delighted, as he realised he could use James's misfortune to his own advantage. James fled to France for help. Louis promised support and encouraged James to invade Ireland, because a war in Ireland would divert troops away from his own struggle in Flanders.

Louis's general was a brilliant mercenary, a Protestant called Schomberg, but Louis made a big mistake. He decided to expel Protestants (Huguenots) from France. Schomberg was very annoyed. He was not going to help a king who punished those with similar beliefs to his and resigned from his position. He was a brilliant leader so, before long, was offered a job by William.

At this time Ireland was in turmoil because native Catholics and Ulster Presbyterians rebelled against the British Crown. They were in Derry under siege when Schomberg landed with William's army at Carrickfergus in 1687 to sort the situation out. This was his first battle, which he won. He was a very different victor from either Queen Elizabeth I or Oliver Cromwell. He was magnanimous, telling defeated people they could go home, or join his army in the fight against James or, if they found that embarrassing, they could join William's army in Flanders. Many Irish Catholics, as well as Ulster Presbyterians, were dissatisfied with King James II as a ruler, so joined William's army. Schomberg didn't attempt to murder everyone, or cause a famine, or destroy the countryside. Instead he hired a Jewish firm, based in Manchester, to buy rations for his army.

Presbyterians would not recognise anyone as head of their church except Jesus Christ, an attitude considered to be treasonable by monarchs of all religious faiths. They wanted the Pope to be recognised as head of the church, or, if they were Protestant, to be recognised in that capacity themselves. As a result, Presbyterians

were in trouble no matter who was on the throne. They were persecuted, forbidden to go to their own church services and their
ministers were under constant threat of death. Failure to attend the
Anglican Church could result in being taken to Dublin and tried
for treason. The penalties varied from being burnt at the stake,
hanged, drawn and quartered or sold as slaves and transported
to the Caribbean and the Carolinas. White descendants of these
slaves still live in the Caribbean today, where they are known as
'Redlegs', because their legs burnt in the sun. They could not work
well in the heat and as a result were not as valuable as black slaves.
As a result of the persecution, many Ulster Presbyterians took
matters into their own hands and emigrated to the New World,
where their descendants are known as Scots Irish.

King William himself landed at Carrickfergus in June 1690 and
marched south to join Schomberg. King James decided that the
best place to make a stand and prepare for battle was beside the
River Boyne, near Drogheda. In those days, the rules of war dictated that when an army made a stand, the opposing army must
fight on that site. William's army hastened south, and the battle
was nearly over before it had begun: William was reconnoitring
one side of the Boyne, unaware that James was hidden by bushes
on the other side. James's artillery got into position and fired a
shot, which killed a man and two horses. A second shot followed
almost immediately. It grazed the bank of the river before bounc-
ing up in the air, hitting William's shoulder.

He got up and remarked, as blood poured out from his
wound, 'That could have been worse. It could have blown my
head off.' He got back on his horse immediately and rode among
his men.

It was very important for morale for William to show his soldiers
that he was all right. They cheered and cheered. On the opposite
bank of the river, King James's soldiers heard the cheering and they
cheered too – because they thought he was dead.

James believed William would attack at a bend in the Boyne
called Rosnaree. William guessed James would station the majority
of his troops there and sent 8,000 soldiers as a decoy, launching his

major attack downstream nearer Drogheda at the ruined village of Oldbridge, so James was outflanked.

According to local folklore, James watched the battle in the grounds of a ruined church at Dunore. When he saw things were going badly, somebody shouted, 'How's the battle going?'

James yelled, 'It's done. It's over. Done! Over! And that's how the village got its name, Dunore.

James deserted his army and fled south towards Dublin, and from that day to this, King James has been called by Irish Catholics, '*Seamus an chaca* (James the shit)'.

At one point in his flight, James slipped and fell while crossing over a gate. The gate was named King's Gate, although the exact location is unknown.

A woman is reputed to have shouted at him, 'Your majesty, you've won the race!'

The Williamites celebrated their victory by striking a medal, which showed James running away from the Battle of the Boyne on one side, while the other shows a deer with wings on its hooves. The medal bore the Latin inscription *pedibus timer addict alas* (fear added wings to his feet). James returned to his cousin Louis in France while the war in Ireland continued for several more years, although the Battle of the Boyne marked the defining moment.

The Battle of the Boyne was a minor skirmish in a bigger struggle played out on the continent of Europe; nevertheless, it is still commemorated annually in Ireland. In Ulster, there are over 3,000 marches each year. As far as the majority of the population is concerned, it's a great family day out, enjoyed by Catholics and Protestants alike. The same Lambeg drums may take part in a St Patrick's Day Parade on 17 March, when they are decorated with shamrocks, and are then festooned with orange lilies for use on 12 July.

The Battle of the Boyne is also commemorated by a Sham Fight, held on 13 July each year in Scarva, which is on the border between Counties Armagh and Down. Hundreds of people attend what has traditionally been a good family day out. It begins when members of the Black Preceptory carry colourful banners depicting biblical scenes and march through the Scarva Demesne up to the big house, where a salute is taken. They are accompanied by bands.

After the parade, King William and King James have a sham fight, during which they fire blank shots at each other. The outcome of the battle is a foregone conclusion: King William always wins, so it must be rather depressing event for his opponent. According to local folklore the actors taking the parts of William and James once really did fall out and fought each other before the big event. This was the only year in which King James won. The organisers

were furious, gave the protagonists a severe telling off and made them repeat the performance to ensure the correct outcome.

Difficulties between actors are not the only ones organisers have encountered. Tradition says King William rode a white horse as a symbol that God was on his side, while King James sat astride a black one. On occasions it has been impossible to find the correct colour of horse, so they've been painted. That's fine, as long as it doesn't rain and wash the paint off, making the horses change colour mid battle!

On Sunday afternoons in the past, before cars became commonplace, people used to dress in their best clothes and walk out from Drogheda to the bridge nearest the town. An obelisk marking the site of the Battle of the Boyne was erected nearby and plaque at the bottom of the obelisk read: 'On a site near here King William III defeated King James II at the head of a popish army.' The obelisk remained there for years, until during the civil war in 1921 when it was blown to smithereens (as were many monuments, including the statue of Queen Victoria in Phoenix Park), the blame for which was attributed to the IRA. Stones from the obelisk were scattered far and wide and were collected by local people for their own personal use. Eventually, years later, a letter from a 91-year-old man appeared in *The Irish Times* confessing that he and his friend, who had been soldiers in the Irish Army, had blown the monument up for a laugh. They knew the IRA would be blamed and had enjoyed their guilty secret for years. He felt now, as he was very old and many years had intervened, that he could safely tell what had really happened.

23

SAINT PATRICK

When I was a wee girl, my Mum used to take me to Cregagh Road Methodist church in East Belfast. One of the clergymen, the Revd R.D.E. Gallagher, told children a story during the service. It was from him that I first heard about the shamrock. To be honest, at the time I was more interested in the shamrock than St Patrick. I didn't think saints were cool. I owe a tremendous debt of gratitude to the late Archbishop Otto Simms, to Dr Tim Campbell, Director of the St Patrick's Centre, Downpatrick, and to Hector McDonnell, for bringing the saint alive as far as I am concerned. I now think of Saint Patrick as a real cool dude with a great sense of humour, a love of craic and a bit of a temper. He said he was 'a miserable sinner', and as another miserable sinner I can empathise with that.

'Oh! No! You can't do that. It's forbidden.' St Patrick's followers looked horrified as he began building a huge bonfire on Slane Hill.

'King Laoghaire'll be furious. He'll send his guards to capture you. They'll take you to King Laoghaire. He'll have you executed!'

'Nobody, and by that we mean NOBODY, is allowed to light a fire on this special morning. All fires must be extinguished, then when the king lights his pascal fire, you're allowed to light yours. That's the rule.'

'If anyone sees smoke, never mind flames, you're dead. Dead, do you hear? Dead!'

St Patrick smiled, 'Where's your faith? God will look after me. I'm wearing the invisible armour He has given me. He'll protect me. I'm safe.'

'It's all right for you to say that. But what about us? Will your God protect us?'

'Of course He will. Come on, quit yer moaning and give us a hand.'

Together they built a huge bonfire and trembled as Patrick torched it, quickly sending billows of smoke into the bright clear air while huge flames burnt brightly.

'That'll put the cat among the pigeons', one of his retainers muttered darkly.

Patrick laughed, 'Aye. It's sure to get a reaction. It's a quick way to get a meeting with the king. Thon bonfire's bound to be seen for miles around. They're sure to see it from Tara.'

'Patrick, you're nuts. You're risking your life!'

'Relax! I've told you, God will look after us. We're safe. Now let's contain our souls in patience while we wait.'

Soldiers arrived shortly afterwards. They were furious. 'What do you think you're up to?' they yelled. 'You're not allowed to light a fire until the king has lit the pascal fire. Why did you go and do that? You're a of right lot of blithering eejits. You'll bring us bring bad luck, so you will. We'll be struck by disease. Our crops will fail and it'll all be your fault, so it will.

'We've been ordered to bring you to the king. He'll have you tortured and executed, so he will. And it'll serve you right. Why in heaven's name did you do such a stupid thing?'

The soldiers grabbed Patrick roughly. 'There's no need to be so rough,' he scolded, then he smiled and said, 'Glory alleluia! Oh! How wonderful! God's filling my head with music.' Much to the astonishment of the people with him, he began to sing the hymn that has since become known as Slane.

Be thou my vision, O Lord of my heart,
naught be all else to me, save that tho art;
thou my best though in the day and the night,
waking or sleeping, thy presence my light.

Be thou my wisdom, be thou my true word,
I ever with thee, and thou with me, Lord;
thou my great Father, and I thy true heir;
thou in me dwelling, and I in thy care.

Be thou my breastplate, my sword for the fight;
be thou my armour, and thou my might;
be thou my soul's shelter, and thou my high tower,
raise thou me heavenward, O Power of my power.

Riches I need not, nor man's empty praise,
thou my inheritance through all my days;
thou and thou only, the first in my heart,
High King of heaven, my treasure thou art.

High King of heaven, when the battle is done,
grant heaven's joys to me, O bright heaven's sun,
Christ of my own heart, whatever befall,
still be my vision, O Ruler of all.

The mouth of one of King Laoghaire's guards fell open in astonishment. He kept watching Patrick in awe. Eventually he turned
to the saint's followers and asked, 'Is yer man half cracked? He
shows no fear. There he is, chittering away in a good imitation of
a songbird, and he's going to see King Laoghaire. I'd rather eat my
eyeballs than face King Laoghaire. Why's yer man so happy when
he's going to be tortured?'

'Yer man, as you call him, says Jesus loves him and protects him.
When I first met him I was like you. I felt he was a first-class loony
but as I got to know him, so many strange things happened that I

believe what he says. Patrick would walk up to the Devil himself
without fear and get away with it.'

'You're joking.'

'No. I'll give you an example. When we arrived in Ireland, the
local big man, a brute of a chief called Dichu, set his killer dog
on us. I was scared stiff, I'm telling ye. The brute ran at Patrick.
I closed my eyes. I couldn't bear to look. I thought it was going
to devour Patrick and he'd end up shredded like mincemeat. He
laughed! Laughed, I'm tellin' ye! Laughed. When I looked up, the
killer dog was standin' with its front paws on Patrick's shoulders
and it was licking his face. Dichu was so impressed that he gave his
barn to us for use as his first church.'

The soldier listened intently to Patrick's life story. How he'd
been the son of a wealthy Roman family who lived in England,
had been captured by pirates and sold as a slave. How he'd herded
sheep on Slemish Mountain in County
Antrim, escaped and boarded a ship, which
had been blown off course and shipwrecked
somewhere on the coast of Europe. How
Patrick had wandered throughout Europe,
becoming a cleric before returning home and
having a vision. As a result of the vision he
sold his birthright and came back to Ireland
to tell people that Jesus loves them.

King Laoghaire's guard was so moved that
he immediately became a Christian.

Patrick was still singing as he was
led into the Great Hall at Tara.
King Laoghaire was enraged.
'HOW DARE YOU LIGHT
A FIRE BEFORE I GIVE
THE SIGNAL?' he
bellowed.

Patrick smiled, 'I
wanted to attract
your attention. I

knew you'd send your guards for me, and I want to tell you about Jesus and how much he loves you.'

'Feel your head. I'm the king! Nobody loves me.'

'I'm sorry you feel that way. You must be very lonely. Everyone needs Jesus. Let me tell you about Him.' Patrick walked quietly and confidently across to the king, sat down beside him and said, 'the Son of God was a man called Jesus. He was born in a stable. He grew up in a very ordinary family in Palestine, in what has been described as a "bad area". When He was thirty years of age, He began performing miracles such as turning water into wine, restoring sight to the blind and enabling the dumb to speak. He was able to cure leprosy, mental illnesses and all sorts of diseases. He was even able to make dead people come to life again.'

'You're joking,' exclaimed King Laoghaire.

'No, I'm not joking,' replied Patrick, 'This is a true story. It's the reason I've come to Ireland. I want to tell people about Jesus and how He died for us. Anyone who believes in Him will go to Heaven after death and have everlasting life.'

'Yer head's a marley! Everyone knows if you're brave and die in battle, you'll go to straight to the Otherworld.'

'And what happens to you if you die in your own bed? Or if you're not brave?' asked Patrick.

King Laoghaire looked puzzled so Patrick continued. 'I suppose heaven is a kind of Otherworld, but it's a world filled with love, not war. Jesus told people about the love His Father has for us. He came to earth and paid a terrible price by being punished for our sins. That means your sins and my sins. He died in the cruelest way possible. His enemies crucified him; that means they attached Him to a wooden cross by hammering nails through His hands and feet and hung Him up. Imagine that! It must have been agonising! When He was dead, His body was taken down from the cross and put into a tomb. He was crucified on a Friday and was up and walking around on the third day after his death. He broke Satan's power so that anyone who believes in Him can enjoy life after death.'

'You mean He went into battle for us.'

'That's exactly right,' Patrick smiled.

'Who are the chiefs in Heaven?'

'God the Father, God the Son, that's Jesus, and the God Holy Spirit. They are the Three in One.'

'What do you mean "the Three in One"? You can't have Three in One. You either have three, or one. That's crazy,' King Laoghaire sounded impatient.

Patrick replied patiently, 'God the Father, Jesus the Son and God Holy Spirit are three individuals who are joined in one.'

'Rubbish!' yelled the king, 'You can't have three people who are joined yet are separate. That's a load of balderdash. You're feeding me a load of baloney. I could do better things than listen to the likes of you.'

Patrick was puzzled. How could he explain the Three in One? He looked down and saw a shamrock at his feet, bent down and picked it up. 'Look,' he said, 'Look at this leaf. Do you see it has three separate parts? Now those three parts are joined at the bottom. Do you see that? It's the same thing with God, Jesus and the Holy Spirit. They are three separate parts yet they are joined.'

At last King Laoghaire understood and became a Christian.

Today, young clover plants are sold as shamrocks. The young leaves do not have the distinctive white markings that are present on mature leaves. St Patrick's shamrock was probably a wood sorrel. They were very common in Ireland at the time; clovers were introduced at a later date.

St Patrick is reputed to have visited County Louth in AD 436 and founded Ardpatrick church and a leper hospital on a hill near Louth village. According to the *Annals of Ulster*, he put the church in the hands of one of his followers, St Mochta, before he left the vicinity and went on to Armagh.

Folklore says when pirates captured St Patrick and sold him into slavery, they also captured his sister, St Lupita. Patrick ended up herding sheep on Slemish Mountain in County Antrim while Lupita was sold to a family in Louth. She had a most unsaintlike life. First of all, she was found in St Melvin's bed, but she insisted she had done nothing wrong; she was simply gaining sanity from his sheets while he was at Mass. She got away with that but later went to work as a prostitute in Armagh. St Patrick was so cross that he got his chariot out and ran it over her three times and killed her. He said Mass for her as her soul entered heaven.

There are conflicting stories about St Patrick: firstly, he was celibate and secondly, he married a *Sheela-na-gig*. *Sheela-na-gigs* may be found in ancient churchyards. She is depicted as a strange female figure with a pained expression and her hands clutching her private female parts below. She represents the ancient pagan goddess of childbirth. Wooden *Sheila-na-gigs* used to be very common in old graveyards, but today only stone ones have survived.

St Patrick's name is preserved in the names of churches he is said to have founded, such as the cathedral at Downpatrick, Seapatrick, County Down on the outskirts of Banbridge and perhaps most famously in Ardpatrick, County Louth. It was here that ancient documents, Saint Patrick's Confession and his Letter to Coroticus, were found. In essence, his confession says he felt he was a miserable sinner who simply wanted to tell the Irish about Jesus. In his Letter to Coroticus, St Patrick expresses the rage he felt after Coroticus kidnapped converts, and I love the wonderful language in which he expresses his anger. He writes that Coroticus and his soldiers were like 'vomit in God's stomach', 'raging wolves devouring God's people', 'greedy animals coveting their neighbours' goods and delighting in murder'. And, if that wasn't enough, he hoped 'they would be killed by viper's tongues, burnt in unquenchable fire or crushed by furious dragons'.

24

GHOSTLY FOOTSTEPS IN CARLINGFORD CASTLE

In days of old, when knights were bold and monkeys ate molasses, Matilda, daughter of the Earl de Lacey, was engaged to be married to Richard de Burgo. The match was approved by King John and her father was delighted. Matilda herself appeared to have what we today would call 'the hots' for Richard. He was a handsome man of aristocratic stock and very wealthy and she looked forward to her wedding day.

Jousting tournaments were common during the thirteenth century, because they gave knights a chance to hone their skills in battle and to show off in front of the ladies. There was great anticipation when a jousting match was arranged during de Whyte, Knight of Ballug Castle's visit to Carlingford. De Whyte had a formidable reputation as a champion and ladies of the court couldn't wait to see him in action. He lived up to his reputation and carried all before him.

De Whyte was a handsome man with beautiful manners and an air of breeding, as well as being well connected. Matilda immediately changed her mind: she no longer wanted to marry de Burgo. She was now in love with de Whyte! He was not nearly as good a catch for the First Lady of the Pale as de Burgo, so Matilda knew her father would not approve – but that only added the attraction of danger to the romance. The two soon became lovers.

Matilda gradually came to realise that everyone in the castle knew about her new lover, except her father, so she arranged to meet de Whyte in the shadow of Carlingford Castle walls.

'Darling,' she whispered, 'This is madness. Complete and utter madness. We'll be caught. Everyone suspects we love each other. Our meetings have become too dangerous!'

De Whyte replied, 'Our love is worth waiting for. You're right. We mustn't see each other again. But if we're patient, things could work out fine. Robert de Mandeville and his family are plotting a rebellion against the king's forces. They realise that if you marry Richard, he becomes the Palatine of Ulster when your father dies. They can't stand that idea.

'I intend to join the De Mandevilles' army along with the knights of Lecale and Dufferin. We'll triumph, then we can get married. You'll wait for me, won't you, darling?'

'I'll never marry Richard. Never, never, never! I hate him!' Matilda swore. 'I'll wait for you until the end of time. If necessary, come and take me by force.'

Unfortunately, de Burco became jealous and suspicious. He watched Matilda carefully, suspecting that she was unfaithful and no longer wanted to be his wife. Her attitude towards him had changed. She was cold and standoffish, not warm and tender. He wanted to get married immediately, but she kept making excuses. One evening he saw her standing in the shadow of the castle walls with de Whyte and was filled with rage. The next morning, he left Carlingford and went to Downpatrick, taking Matilda and her father with him.

A knight told de Burco of the plot to overthrow King John and how de Whyte was involved. De Burco became even angrier, gathered his army and headed to the Castle of Ballug, which he took by surprise. He came face to face with de Whyte during the fight and the two men eyed each other. De Whyte saw the loathing on de Burco's face and realised his liaison with Matilda was no longer a secret. A deadly struggle began, which went on and on and on until de Burco slipped and fell. De Whyte raised his dagger to slit de Burco's throat just as his men-at-arms came into the room. One of them caught de Whyte's arm as it descended and saved de Burco's life.

De Whyte was bound, carried to Carlingford Castle in triumph and thrown into the dungeon. De Burco decided to find out how far his relationship with Matilda had gone. Was she guilty of more than a mild flirtation? Had she? Had she? Had she …? What had she been up to? He had de Whyte taken to the torture chamber and his minions did their worst. They used thumbscrews, scourges and the rack. De Whyte's thumbs were broken. He was bleeding badly as he was torn joint from joint so he could no longer walk and resembled a floppy rag doll. Every time he lost consciousness he was revived and the torture began again, but he did not utter one word to implicate Matilda before he died.

A trial was held and de Whyte was sentenced to death by hanging. Thankfully he died before he could be executed. De Burco, in a final act of vengeance, had the body hung out in chains from the castle's battlements.

Matilda was told of de Whyte's death, but not how he died. After a brief period of mourning, she did what her father wanted and married de Burco. That's when the trouble began. Ghostly footsteps were heard resounding round the dungeon, ascending and descending steps, corridors and parapets. Terrified sentinels carried out their duties in fear and trembling. Matilda heard the footsteps and was petrified. They appeared to follow her. She screamed. There was something menacing about the sound.

'Revenge! Revenge! Revenge!' they seemed to whisper.

People said the tortured soul of the murdered Knight of Ballug haunted the castle and Matilda was told the truth about her lover's death. She was so angry that she left her husband and went to live with friends in Dublin. Richard was distraught. He felt very lonely as he sat alone each night, wishing he could hear Matilda's footsteps returning to him, but all he heard was the ghostly sound of his murdered victim.

A soft footfall
In the lonely hall,

Steps approaching,
Are these for me
Coming gently, coming fast
And why not may such things be?

Eventually Matilda forgave Richard and returned, and the couple went to live at Downpatrick, well away from the sound of ghostly footsteps. In 1305, de Burco tried to make restitution for de Whyte's murder by founding the Dominican Abbey in Carlingford. However, the ghostly footsteps continually haunted Carlingford Castle until after de Burco's death. On 6 June 1333, Robert de Mandeville, warden of Carrickfergus Castle, murdered Matilda's son, William, who had inherited the title Earl of Ulster. His death avenged the Knight of Ballug and the ghostly footsteps in Carlingford Castle disappeared.

25

SAINT PATRICK
AND THE SNAKES

(Reproduced with the kind permission of Crawford Howard)

You've heard of the snakes in Australia,
You've heard of the snakes in Japan,
You've heard of the rattler – that old Texas battler,
Whose bite can mean death to a man.
They've even got snakes in auld England,
Nasty adders all yellow and black,
But in Erin's fair Isle, we can say with a smile,
They're away and they're not coming back.

Now years ago things was quite different,
There were serpents all over the place.
If ye climbed up a ladder ye might meet an adder,
Or a cobra might leap at yer face.
If ye went for a walk up the Shankill,
Or a dander along Sandy Row,
A flamin' great python would likely come writhin'
An' take a great lump outta yer toe.

There once was a guy called St Patrick,
A preacher of fame and renown
An' he hoisted his sails and came over from Wales,

To convert all the heathen in Down.
An' he herpled about through the country
With a stick and a big pointy hat,
An' he kept a few sheep that he sold on the cheap,
But sure there's no money in that.

He was preachin' a sermon in Comber
And getting quite carried away
When he mentioned that Rome had once been his home
And that was the wrong thing to say,
For he felt a sharp bite on his cheekbone
An stuck a han' up til his bake
An the thing that had lit on his gub and had bit,
Was a wee Presbyterian snake.

Now the snake slithered down from the pulpit,
Expecting St Patrick to die,
But yer man was no dozer – he lifted his crozier,
An' belted the snake in the eye.
Says he to the snake, 'Listen legless,
Ye'd better take yerself off
If ye think that that trick will work on St Patrick,
Ye must be far worser than daft.'

So the snake slithered home in a temper,
An gathered his friends all around,
Says he, 'Listen mates, we'll get on our skates,
I reckon it's time to leave town.
It's no fun when ye bite a big fella,
An' sit back and expect him to die,
And he's so flamin' quick with yon big crooked stick
That he hits ye a dig in the eye.'

So a strange sight confronted St Patrick
When he woke the very next day.
The snakes, with long faces, were all packing their cases,

And heading for Donegal Quay.
Some got on cheap flights to Majorca
And some booked apartments in Spain.
They were all headin' out and there wasn't a doubt
They weren't comin' back again.

So the reason the snakes left auld Ireland
(an' this is no word of a lie),
They all went to places to bite people's faces
And be reasonably sure that they'd die.
An' the auld snakes still caution their grandsons,
'For God's sake beware of St Pat
An take yourselves off if you see his big staff,
An' his coat an' his big pointy hat!'

Crawford Howard

26

SAINT BRIGID

I am indebted to Dara Vallely, one of the Armagh Rhymers, who first told me of St Brigid's association with Faughart (north of Dundalk) and about the healing stones situated there.

While visiting Faughart I met Sister Betty, a nun who had recently returned from Africa. She told me about the nearby St Brigid's Well, which is in the graveyard of Dulargy and we visited it together.

There is a lot of folklore about the relationship between St Brigid and St Patrick, although there is no evidence that they were even born in the same century. The oral tradition states that St Patrick, St Brigid and St Columncille are buried in the same grave in the churchyard of Downpatrick Cathedral.

St Brigid, the daughter of a wealthy man and his slave, was born a few miles north of Dundalk at Faughart. Her mother had been sent to fetch a pitcher of milk and managed to give birth on the threshold of her master's dwelling without spilling a drop. Brigid was immediately bathed in milk, then – following the ancient tradition – drops of milk were sprinkled in every corner of the room to purify it. But, the saint suffered from an easily upset stomach so she couldn't drink ordinary milk. Instead she was always fed by milk from a pure white cow.

A shrine has been built in her honour among the trees at Faughart, and site is now almost aggressively Christian, although it dates back to pagan times. A stream rushes down the mountainside at Faughart and there is a series of healing stones along the boundary of a field on the Dundalk side of the shrine. Each stone is shaped like the organ it is said to treat and is clearly labelled. There is an eye stone, a back stone, a knee stone, a foot stone and so on.

According to folklore, if you want to receive a blessing from a specific site, you must make an offering in return. People tied small offerings, such as pieces of cloth, ribbons or paper on things like trees or nearby fences. This practice is still common, although I have never seen anyone actually doing it. When the Catholic Church built a structure nearby to facilitate mass, the ancient practice of leaving offerings appeared to shift to St Brigid's Well in Dulargy graveyard; the evergreen bush beside the well became covered in a multitude of offerings. More recently a few offerings have appeared again on the barbed-wire fence beside the healing stones.

On St Brigid's Eve (31 January), St Brigid's spirit is said to come back to earth and dip her feet into a stream, bringing spring. According to folklore, St Patrick was very annoyed when he heard how St Bridget turned winter into spring and decided to go one better. He brought summer into existence by turning the stone on St Patrick's Day and made it possible to predict the weather. If it rains on St Patrick's Day, it will rain for a further forty days.

Apparently, St Patrick was jealous of St Brigid. She annoyed him by wandering around the countryside helping the poor, healing the sick and performing miracles. He reckoned she should stay in her nunnery and leave important jobs to men, such as himself.

Fishermen regard St Brigid's Day (*Fhéile Bhríde*) as the start of the fishing season. They are very superstitious and think it's a waste of time going fishing if they see a red-haired woman, a bare foot, a hare, a priest or a fox on the way to their boat.

If you dislike a fisherman and want to curse him for a season say:

> May there be a fox on your fishing hook,
> A hare on your bait,
> And may you kill no fish until St Brigid's Day.

At one time there were no herbs growing in Irish streams. One day a band of holy virgins asked, 'Mother, why are there no water herbs growing in the streams of Ireland for holy men to eat?'

St Brigid thought, 'They're right,' and spent the whole night praying. The next day, people found the streams full of watercress.

Some lepers came to St Brigid, saying they were very thirsty and would like a drink of ale. She was a very generous person and was upset because she didn't have any. She saw some water being prepared for baths, blessed it with the power of faith and promptly turned it into an excellent ale.

St Brigid's generosity worried her father, because she gave so much away that he was frightened of being ruined. One day he took her to a castle and tried to sell her as a servant to the king. He left her sitting outside in his chariot. A poor man came up to her and pleaded for money. She didn't have any so gave him her father's sword, which was very valuable, being worth the equivalent of ten cows.

The dandelion is associated with St Brigid. It is called *Caiserarbhan* in Irish, meaning 'the knotted plant of Bride', referring to its serrated leaves. It begins blooming around St Brigid's Day (1 February) and produces a milk-like sap believed to give nourishment to early lambs. St Brigid is thought to be an adaption of ancient Celtic goddess Brighid, who may have had an indirect connection with the sun. St Brigid herself was often likened to the sun. The dandelion looks like the sun and appears at the start of the Celtic spring, so is an appropriate plant to represent both the goddess and the saint. Dandelions are known as 'Pee-the-Beds' because of their diuretic effect. As a young child I was frightened to stand on a dandelion in case it made me wet my bed.

Brigid went to the King of Leinster and asked him to grant land to her monastery so she could have more sheep and cows to produce more milk, cheese and meat for the poor. The king refused, but she pleaded with him. He became fed up and snarled, 'Alright! You can have as much land as your cloak can cover.'

She smiled and said, 'That's great! Thank you.'

Four nuns each grabbed a corner of the cloak and ran as fast as they could in opposite directions. As the nuns ran, the cloak grew and grew and grew until it covered a square mile. The king became alarmed in case it covered the whole of his kingdom and shouted, 'Stop! You may have all the land under your cloak.' St Brigid agreed.

There is a dark crimson piece of cloth measuring 54.5cm x 64cm (21in x 25in) in the cathedral of St Saviour in Brugge, Belgium known as *La Manteline de St Brigide d'Ireland* (the Mantle of St Brigid of Ireland). The outer surface is covered with tufts of curly wool, making it look like a sheep's fleece. It was given to the church by Princess Gunhild, who had two brothers, Harold (who was killed at the Battle of Hastings in 1066) and Leofwine. These brothers stayed with Dermot, King of Leinster when they attempted to raise an army. It is very likely that they visited St Brigid's birthplace at Faughart and her cathedral in Kildare, so it is possible that they really did obtain a piece of her cloak and give it to the Cathedral of St Saviour in Brugge, Belgium, although by that time she was dead and her remains had been relocated to Down about 170 years earlier.

THE GHOST IN THE GRAVEYARD OF KILEAVY OLD CHURCH

I got this story from Linda Ballard, who was Curator of Textiles in the Ulster Folk and Transport Museum at the time. She was also instrumental, along with Liz Weir, in encouraging a revival of the traditional art of storytelling in Ireland.

Dara Vallely, one of the Armagh Rhymers, told me how the ghost in this story returned in the 1990s, indirectly causing the death of two young people. This event was reported in the local press.

Try telling this story on a dark night by fire or candlelight. Keep your voice peaceful, calm and as quiet as possible then, when the ghost appears, move suddenly and shout loudly. Listeners nearly jump out of their skins!

I love this story because it expresses a great truth. In Ireland we are supposed to fit neatly into one of two boxes, depending on politics and religious faith. That's true for some, but not for all. The vast majority of people tend to be ignored because crossing boundaries is not newsworthy.

Anne was thought to be a good catch. All the fellas were crazy about her. She'd make a great wife, so she would. She had a big broad back that could pull a plough, and she was so tall she could eat hay out of a loft like a horse. Her shoulders were broad and muscular, and she was so strong that she could carry two buckets of water. In the past, Irish men were not interested in a woman's appearance. All they wanted was a big strong wife who could work hard around a farm. Anne fitted the bill and, best of all, she was an only child. Her parents were dead and she lived with her granny on a tidy wee farm that she would eventually inherit.

The cottage in which Anne lived was near the gates of Kileavy old church. Every Saturday night, Anne used to dress in her best and walk, alone, to the *ceili* house behind the graveyard. She enjoyed a bit of craic, loved dancing and had a good singing voice. When the *ceili* was over, she walked over to the graveyard's wall and used spaces in the worn brickwork to climb to the top and jump down among the headstones. She didn't believe in ghosts and was happy taking the short cut home. The boys did their best to persuade her that she should have company but she always refused, saying, 'No, thank you. I'm perfectly capable of getting myself home. Sure, it's only two shakes of a lamb's tail. I'll just take my usual shortcut through the graveyard.'

'You should know by now, I've no time for fellas. I've a farm to run. Being walked home is the thin end of a wedge leading to marriage. I've no intention of ever doing anything so foolish as getting hitched. I've enough to do washing my own dirty socks without washing those of a husband too. Thank you kindly, but the answer's no.'

The more Anne played hard to get, the keener the boys were to catch her. One night, they planned a wicked trick. Two of the boys thought they'd frighten her by dressing up as a ghost. Perhaps then she'd swoon with fear and fall into their arms. It was worth a try.

Anne heard her friends giggling and guessed they were planning some sort of mischief. 'I bet,' she thought, 'those big fools are going to pretend they're ghosts. I don't know how many times I've told them I don't believe in ghosts. I'll fool them, so I will. I'll go home by a different path. It's a cold night and if they freeze to death among the tombstones, it'll serve them right, so it will.'

She sauntered slowly over to the graveyard wall, climbed on to the top and jumped down. The moon shone bright as she wended her way down a different path, one she had never walked before. She moved slowly as she was showing off, demonstrating how brave and sensible she was and how she didn't need a man. She wasn't frightened of anything, so she wasn't. She wasn't like the majority of girls. They were lily-livered. She was strong and self-sufficient. Then OHHHHHHHHHHHHH! A large figure, dressed in white, suddenly appeared from behind a tombstone. Anne nearly jumped out of her skin, then laughed, 'Good on ye, lads. That was a good trick, I'll grant ye. Ye made me jump, but I don't believe in ghosts. You know that and ye don't scare me!' And with that she pulled the sheet away and ran laughing towards her home.

All her friends were sitting down round the fire with old granny. Anne told them how the boys had tried to frighten her in the graveyard, showed them the sheet and threw it into the corner. They laughed and thought how brave and clever she was.

There was a funny smell in the room but everyone was too polite to mention it.

About an hour later, two very cold boys entered. 'Thon was a dead loss, so it was,' one of them said,' Somebody must have gone home a different way than usual. We're frozen stiff and we didn't see hilt nor hair of a soul.'

'Nonsense,' snapped Anne. 'A joke's a joke, but you are going a bit too far. I did see you. I pulled a sheet off you!'

'No you didn't! You didn't come anywhere near us. You mustn't have gone your usual way home.'

'That's true, 'Anne replied, 'I guessed you were up to something. Quit your codding. You must have seen me, then gone round the other way and got ahead of me. When you jumped out from behind a headstone, I pulled the sheet off you.'

'Oh no you didn't; we have our sheet here.'

Anne got up, stamped her foot in a rage and shouted, 'You're carrying things a bit too far. I've got the sheet here.' She went into the corner where she'd flung the sheet and picked it up.

Granny went very white. 'I think we should have a look at those sheets,' she said as she did a very extravagant thing. She fetched a candle and lit it. Candles were very expensive in those far-off days. After dark, people used light from the fire and simple rush lights they made themselves.

When they examined the sheets, they saw the boys' sheet was clean, pristine and had folds left from when it had been ironed. The sheet Anne held up to the light was stained and slimy, with a few leaves and a big fat slug stuck to it. It bore a faint stench of decay.

'OOOOOOOH!' she yelled, 'That's horrible. What should I do? Ugh! Throw it on the fire?'

'No,' said one of the girls very quietly, 'that's the last thing you should do. I've heard if you steal something that belongs to the dead you have to give it back, or be cursed. Don't do anything until we get some advice. Destroying anything that belongs to the dead could result in your death.'

'But I didn't steal anything,' sobbed Anne. 'I thought I was confounding those stupid boys, who were out to frighten me.'

'Anne, we know you wouldn't steal anything, but you took that shroud. That's what it is: a shroud, not a sheet. You have it. That's what matters. You must give it back to its owner.'

'How do I give it back?'

'I honestly don't know. Let's go and tell the priest everything. He's a very decent wee man. He knows all about ghosts. He'll help you.'

'But it's very late,' Anne protested, 'I can't go disturbing him at this time of night. It's not fair.'

'Anne,' said one of the boys, 'I think you should go immediately. The priest won't mind. This is an emergency. We don't know how long you've got before the curse works, or even if you are cursed.'

'But,' said Anne, 'I don't even go to his church. It's an imposition. I'm a Presbyterian, not a Catholic.'

A response came quickly. 'That doesn't matter. Your minister's a fine practical sort of fella, but he's not into ghosts.'

Anne agreed and the group of young people set off down the road to the priest's house and told him the whole story. He was very upset. 'Yes,' he said, 'you're right. Anne's in great danger. We've got to get that shroud back to its owner. Anne, I suggest you hang it on the hedge nearest the graveyard and with any luck the ghost will reclaim it and the danger'll be over. If it's still there in the morning, come back to me and I'll tell you what to do next. But let's pray that's not necessary.'

'What happens if somebody steals it?' Anne asked nervously.

'That's their problem, not yours. The curse will leave you and fall on them.' The young people did what the priest suggested and went home to bed.

Poor Anne lay awake all night, praying, crying and shivering with fear. At first light she crept out of bed, went to the window and peered out. Her heart sank. The shroud was still hanging on the hedge. She dressed quickly and went back to the priest's house. He saw her coming, opened the door and said, 'Oh dear. I take it from the look on your face the shroud's still there.'

Anne burst into tears. He put his arm around her shoulders and drew her gently into his house. 'I'm so sorry,' he said, 'This is going to be difficult and very frightening. You must find a new-born baby and take it into the graveyard at about 10 o'clock at night. The evil spirit cannot touch an innocent child, so you will be safe. Any baby up until the age of about two years will do, but the younger the better. Wrap yourself, and it, up warmly then keep the baby tight against your body and hold the shroud out with your other hand so it can be clearly seen. The ghost will have to reclaim it and you will be free from the curse. You must go alone. Anyone accompanying you will die and the ghost will kill you if you go alone and aren't protected by a baby.'

Anne spent a miserable day attempting to 'borrow' a baby. Nobody would lend her one. Parents were, understandably, reluctant to allow their precious child into a graveyard late at night. Nine o'clock at night found Anne miserably crying at the fireside with her granny. 'It's not fair. It's not my fault the boys played such a wicked trick on me. I don't want to die. I'm too young.'

'I don't want you to die,' old granny howled, 'I'd never manage the farm on my own. I'll die of starvation.'

The door opened and in came the Presbyterian clergyman with his wife and baby daughter, a beautiful baby, who was eleven months of age and had fair curly hair. 'Anne dear,' he said, 'We're so sorry to have been so thoughtless and to have allowed you to be so frightened. The truth of the matter is we don't like the idea of our wee baby being taken into the graveyard. We were hoping somebody else would lend you one but that obviously hasn't happened, so you can take our daughter.'

'Do you mean it?' Anne gasped through her tears.

'Yes dear,' the wife replied. 'We mean it. We're really sorry for your trouble. Now, come on, let's have a wee drink of buttermilk and a bit of soda bread. You could have a long night ahead of you and we don't want you to faint for lack of nourishment, do we? I'm sure eating's the last thing you feel like doing but, come on, force it down you, then we'll help you get ready. We'll stay here with granny and pray for you until you get back.'

Just before ten o'clock Anne dressed warmly, wrapped the baby in a woollen tweed rug and headed towards the churchyard. She shuddered as she lifted the shroud off the hedge. The baby seemed unconcerned. She gurgled, then closed her eyes and fell asleep. Anne cuddled her close and walked up and down and up and down. For the first time in her life Anne saw the graveyard as a dark, menacing, evil place. She shivered with a mixture of cold and fear. She heard eleven o'clock, twelve o'clock, one o'clock, two o'clock, three o'clock, four o'clock. Her heart was in despair. 'This isn't working,' she thought, 'the priest must be mistaken. There's no sign of the ghost. It's not coming back. It'll soon be dawn. I'm doomed. Doomed! It's not fair. I'm going to die because the boys played a stupid trick.'

Tears ran down her face at the thought, when suddenly a ghastly figure jumped out from behind a headstone.

Anne screamed and jumped backwards, while the babe woke and yelled lustily. The figure grabbed the shroud and put it on. A decayed finger with the flesh hanging off it appeared around the edge of the shroud and pointed at Anne.

'If it weren't for that innocent child,' an evil voice cackled, 'I'd kill you.' With that it disappeared.

Anne sobbed with relief and fear as she stumbled to the gate where she found granny, the cleric and his wife praying in the lane. 'We heard you scream and came to see what we could do,' granny explained as they helped Anne back into the house.

The next Saturday night, when one of the fellas asked Anne if he could see her home, she thought about it for a minute then said, 'Yes. That would be rather nice.'

She was right; it was the thin end of the wedge. She did end up marrying him and washing his smelly socks. She had nineteen children and eventually grew to love his socks.

28

THE PROLEEK
DOLMEN

I know this story sounds unlikely but it is true. It is what I experienced.

I have visited the Sumter Campus of the University of South Carolina on many occasions. I was their first Storyteller in Residence and they awarded me a silver medal for my services. After my first visit I stayed with Dr Jack Doyle and his charming wife, Annette. They were extremely kind and I had what Americans refer to as 'a blast'.

Tom Prewett was, at that time, Sumter Campus's publicity officer. Jack and he said they would love the experience of storytelling in Ireland and I invited them both to come to and stay with me. The three of us enjoyed storytelling together and sightseeing. During their visit I took them to see the Proleek Dolmen in the grounds of the Ballymascalon Hotel near Dundalk. Dolmens are ancient graves said to represent a door into the Otherworld. Two types of dolmen are found along the path close to the golf course in the grounds of the hotel. There is a small, not-very-spectacular-looking wedge tomb and a huge, impressive portal dolmen known as the Proleek Dolman.

The Proleek Dolman predates the pyramids of Egypt and consists of three large rocks, standing on their ends with a magnificent capstone weighing 40 tons. If you use your imagination, it does have a passing resemblance to a doorway and it's easy to imagine passing through to the Otherworld. The top of the dolmen is covered in small stones. Tradition says if pick up a stone, make a wish and throw the stone up on to the top of the dolmen your wish will come true – if it stays there.

Jack, Tom and I each picked up a stone and threw it up on top of the capstone. My stone fell down immediately, as did Tom's, but Jack's stayed in place. Tom and I laughed and said, 'Well, it looks as if the dolman doesn't like us. We've no chance of our wishes coming true, but you're all right, Jack.'

There was no reply. We turned round and looked at Jack. He was white and shaking. 'That thing's evil,' he gasped. 'Get me out of here. Quick.'

Tom and I were very amused; it was a beautiful day. There was no sign of anything evil. The surrounding country was quiet and peaceful.

'You two stay there if you like,' Jack insisted. 'I'm telling you, that thing's evil. I don't know what's wrong with it. All I can say is, I don't like it and I need a drink. I'm getting out of here, now, and I'm never going to throw a stone at that thing again.'

And with that he started to trudge back up the path leading to the Ballymascalon Hotel, where we bought him a pint of Guinness.

Tom and I teased Jack without mercy after that incident, but the next time I visited the Proleek Dolman I threw a stone up on to the top of the capstone. It stayed in place. I felt as if the capstone had sucked my stone towards it. It was a strange, strange sensation and I, like Jack, was frightened. I am never going to throw a stone at the capstone of the Proleek Dolmen ever again. There is something there I don't understand and I don't believe in mucking around with things like that. And I apologise sincerely to Jack for laughing at him.

29

LASSARA'S LEAP FROM NARROW WATER CASTLE

I first heard this traditional story from my old friend, the late Joan Gaffney, who wrote hilarious comic verse and was a gifted storyteller.

> Anon in sweet and plaintive lay,
> His fingers o'er the harp strings stray,
> And lady lists in pleased surprise,
> And brighter beam her sparkling eyes,
> The harper's glance is o'er her cast,
> And loud her heart beats, quick and fast.

Lassara felt restless, ill at ease and dissatisfied with life.

'What's wrong with me?' she wondered. 'I'm a Princess of Iveagh, a daughter of the MacGuinness. I'm surrounded by every comfort. I live in a dun, not a miserable rat-ridden hovel. I've plenty to eat and drink as well as slaves to wait on me. I don't have to labour in the fields. A good marriage has been arranged for me. What more do I want? Why am I unhappy? I should be thankful, not miserable. I must cheer up. I need a good shake-up. I know what I'll do.

I'll take myself off for a walk. It's a beautiful morning, the birds are singing and it should be impossible to be miserable on such a day.'

She walked out of the dun and down the road leading to the nearby glen. Then she heard it. Beautiful, mysterious, wistful music drifting softly through the trees. She felt drawn towards it. 'That must be the mad harper,' she thought. She had heard of the harper, who had suddenly appeared as if from nowhere, and spent the winter entertaining local warriors. She hadn't seen him but had heard others gossiping, wondering where he had come from, and why he stayed. Some said he was mad; others that he was simply a talented musician who liked to seek out solitary places and be alone to compose music.

Lassara followed the sound as she drifted through the trees. She found the harper in a clearing, sitting with his back to her. The melancholy notes surrounding him pulled at her very heartstrings, so she sat down on the grass and watched and listened. There was no doubt about it. He was a musical genius. The harp was almost singing, with its voice echoing the sad sounds her soul was sighing.

At last the harper stopped playing, stood up, lifted his harp and turned round. He gasped when he caught sight of her. She stood up, gazed into his eyes and was spellbound. He walked towards her in wonderment.

'Fair lady, you must be the Princess of Iveagh. I've heard about you. What are you doing here so far from the dun?'

'I went for a walk and heard your music,' Lassara replied, 'and felt drawn towards it. It seemed to echo my feelings. It's so wistful and full of longing. Why do you make your harp make sounds like that?'

'Fair lady, I can see into the future. Unfortunately this beautiful place is going to be encompassed by war. Dark clouds are gathering.' He looked deep into her eyes, 'Come,' he said, 'come away with me. Your life is in danger. I'm willing to leave my people, take you as my bride and fly away. We'll seek refuge on Loch Ochter's distant isle. We'd be happy and safe there. What do you think? I could get things arranged for early tomorrow morning then call you by playing my harp. Follow the sound and we'll go together to the Nun's Island [it now forms part of the Louth mainland and is the wooded height jutting into the river near the ferry]. The sisters have left, but an aged *cleireach* lives there and he's sure to agree to marry us.'

Lassara agreed.

At daybreak, the alluring music sounded. The harper's call was more irresistible than ever. Lassara turned to her women and said, 'I'm going to visit the holy shrine.' She left the dun without causing any suspicion and was soon in the glen by the harper's side.

At dusk that evening they took a skiff and drifted with the ebb tide downriver. It was a very dark night. The skiff was borne silently by the swift current towards Narrow-water Castle. The young people held their breath: they hoped to drift past without being spotted. Once the danger of the castle had been avoided, it was an easy journey to Nun's Island and a marriage ceremony in the hermit's cell. Unfortunately they were spotted by the keen eyes of the sentry on duty.

'Who goes there?' he shouted. The young couple quivered with fear but did not answer. The sentry lifted his *arquebus* [an early type of portable gun supported on a tripod by a hook or forked rest]. There was a flash of flame as a shot sounded. The harper gasped in agony and fell over the side of the skiff, clasping his harp to his breast as he sank beneath the dark waters.

Lassara fainted and fell to the bottom of the boat, which drifted helplessly downstream. Meanwhile, the black shadow of a boat, manned by soldiers from the castle's garrison, slid out from under the castle's walls. It followed Lassara downstream and they captured her. They were delighted to recognise the Princess of Iveagh, daughter of the MacGuinness of the Rinn. She would make a valuable hostage. They locked her up in the damp mouldy dungeon of the castle. It was as silent as a tomb but she had one great comfort. Every night, she heard harp strings sounding in the dash of the waves against the outer walls of the castle and knew the spirit of her lover was serenading her.

Lassara was very beautiful and the castle's warden fell in love with her. But, she hated him. He asked her to marry him and she refused. He was furious. How dare Lassara refuse the offer of freedom that marriage to him would bring? It was an insult.

'I'll give you a week to accept my proposal or I'll have you tortured and put to death,' he threatened.

Lassara wisely did nothing to annoy the warden during her week's grace. When she heard his heavy footsteps on the last day, she flattened her body against the wall beside the door. As the warden entered her cell, she darted out behind him and raced up the dark stairway. Up, up and up she went until she reached the top of the building. She rushed over to the ramparts and looked down. It was a wild night, but she could hear the heavy thud of the warden's feet behind her. The wind howled, trees rocked and waves swirled below. Suddenly the harper rose above the waves. He held out his arms.

'Jump, Lassara, jump, darling! Jump!' he called.

Lassara jumped.

From that day to this, on wild stormy nights when the waves are swirling around the base of Narrow-water Castle, the plaintive sounds of a harp can be heard. Watch carefully and you will see a slender white figure appearing on the ramparts before descending from the top of Narrow-water Castle into the wild waters below.

OLIVER CROMWELL'S
SIEGE OF DROGHEDA

Mr and Mrs S.C. Hall were married during the early 1800s and spent their honeymoon touring Ireland. It must have been a strange sort of honeymoon because on their return to London, the couple wrote a comprehensive guide to Ireland – *Hall's Ireland: its Scenery, Character* &c published in London by Hall, Virtue & Co., 25 Paternoster Row. It is partly from this work that I discovered information about Oliver Cromwell's actions in Drogheda.

Cromwell is immortalised in Irish Folklore as a ruthless general, who hated the Irish and caused a 'famine the likes of which has never been seen'. His memory is such that today, over 400 years later, it is still possible to hear angry people say, 'May the curse of Cromwell be upon you.'

Trouble began in 1641 during the reign of King Charles I and erupted again in 1649. The Protestant Ulster-Scots population were enraged by the treatment they received from the government. The Ulster-Scots, or Scots Irish, as they are called in America, were forced to flee from Scotland because they were being persecuted for their beliefs. They were a stubborn lot and refused to recognise any monarch as head of their Church. That applied to pope, kings and dictators. The only person they would recognise was Jesus Christ, a frame of mind which did not go down well with the authorities.

In 1637, staunch Ulster Presbyterians were forced to take what they referred to as the 'Black Oath', forcing them to swear to recognise the king as head of the church. Refusal resulted in being sent to Dublin for trial and, if found guilty, punished by being burnt at the stake, hanged, drawn and quartered, or transported to Bermuda as slaves.

Many Ulster-Scots emigrated to America because of the Black Oath. They took their tools, their language and their skill with them and had a profound effect: nineteen American presidents have been of Ulster-Scots descent.

In some ways during this period, Presbyterian Ulster-Scots were treated worse than native Irish Catholics, who did not have to take the Black Oath.

Cromwell decided it would be wise to squash the uprising in Ireland. He led his army of 8,000 foot soldiers, 4,000 men on horseback, £20,000 cash and a large number of the weapons of war to Tredagh (the ancient name of Drogheda). It had a garrison of 2,500 men and 300 horse under the command of the governor, Sir Arthur Aston.

Cromwell laid siege to the old town and soldiers in the garrison swore they'd rather die than surrender. They managed to fight off two attacks but Cromwell succeeded on the third assault attempt. Aston and his men fought bravely, forcing the conquerors to win ground inch by inch, with numerous losses on both sides. After the battle, Cromwell gave what folklore records as his 'infernal order' for a general and indiscriminate massacre, which he recorded on 17 September 1649 in a letter to the Speaker, William Lenthall.

> The governor, Sir Arthur Aston, and divers considerable officers, being there, our men getting at them were ordered by me to put them all to the sword, and indeed, being in the heat of action, I forbade them to spare any that were in arms in the

town, and I think that night they put to the sword about two
thousand men; divers of the officers and men being fled over the
bridge into another part of the town, where about one hundred
of them possessed Saint Peter's Church, some the west gate, and
others the round tower, next the gate, called Saint Sunday's;
these being summoned to yield to mercy, refused, whereupon
I ordered the steeple of S. Peter's to be fired, when one of them
was heard to say in the midst of the flames, 'God damn me!
God confound me! I burn! I burn!' the next day the other towers
were summoned, in one of them which was about six or seven
score, but they refuse to yield themselves, and we knowing
hunger must compel them, set only a good guard to secure them
from running away, until their stomachs were come down; from
one of the said towers, notwithstanding their condition, they
killed and wounded some of our men; when they submitted
themselves, their officers were knocked on the head, and every
tenth man of the soldiers killed, and the rest shipped for the
Barbadoes.

When Acton was slaughtered, Cromwell's soldiers fought over
his artificial leg. They thought it was either made of gold, or had
a cavity filled with gold coins. They were mistaken, so chopped
it up.

St Peter's church was Anglican – that is, it was of the same religious denomination as Cromwell himself. It was built of stones,
with the exception of the wooden steeple. Cromwell originally
planned to blow the church up, as an open subterranean tunnel
went under it. He put explosives in place but changed his mind
and decided to set fire to the steeple instead. When the building
caught fire, people rushed out the door and were slaughtered, all
except one man. He jumped from the tower and broke his legs and
for some unknown reason the soldiers spared his life.

Cromwell continued to slaughter residents of Drogheda for five
days, after which he went for a walk through the streets. He found
them covered in blood and corpses and was completely unmoved
until he saw the dead body of a young mother stretched out on the

road. A very young baby was attempting to feed at her breast. After that he left Drogheda and went to wage war elsewhere.

People working in Millmount Museum have since recorded hearing the ghost of a young baby crying. Is it the same baby? Nobody knows.

GLOSSARY

Amadan: an individual who struggles educationally and/or clumsy
Auld: old
Baloney: nonsense
Blatter: thump, hit hard
Big girl's blouse: an individual who is useless
Brúg na Bóinne: New Grange
Bonkers: mad
Blithering: talking nonsense
Balderdash: nonsense
Craic: fun, chat
Croachan: ancient war cry, also the name of Queen Maeve's dun
Clatter: make a noise with
Cissy: timid individual
Codding: joking
Could sit up and eat an egg: feeling better/well
Couldn't hit a cow up the ass with a bake-board: poor aim
Chittering: light chatter
Couldn't catch yer granny in a field: slow runner
Cud: could
Dead on: excellent, 100 per cent
Devil's imp: little rascal
Dun Dealgan: Dundalk, Cúchulainn's home
Dun: dwelling of powerful individual

Edjiot: idiot

Eight sheets to the wind: inebriated

Eyes out on stalks: astonished

Feisty: chilly, lively

Gae bolga: special spear given to Cúchulainn by Skya. If it hit an adversary, death was inevitable because it travelled up and destroyed blood vessels

Geassa: very serious promise, or oath. If it was broken, a curse came into play

Guldered: shouted loudly

Half a sandwich short of a picnic: stupid

Headbin: mad, not wise

How's about ye: hello

Head's cut: whatever you are doing or saying is not wise

Head banger: individual who is mad

Half cracked: unwise

Harden their groins: will be painful

I cud lick moisture off a cow's bum through a hedge: I am very thirsty

Jumped up nothin': from a low socio-economic background now living at a higher level

Keen: a type of singing often heard at wakes

Knock the melt out of: fight, beat up

Leanhaun Shee: lovely fairy mistress who enables her lovers to write beautiful poetry but causes their death and makes them walk the earth after death as a miserable ghost

Laugh yer leg off: hearty laugh

Leprechaun: fairy shoemaker who is the size of a child between two and six years of age

Lily-livered: cowardly

Look at the cut of: look at the style/attitude of

Looney: mad person

Lorney bless us: exclamation

Lugh: the sun god, said to be the father of Cúchulainn. Lugh's name is immortalised in the names of various places such as County Louth, London, Leicester etc.

Lukin' ye: searching/looking for you

Moseying: engaging in aimless activity

May yer cess never go sour: may nothing unpleasant ever happen to you

May the hens of hell roost on yer chest: may you spend a long time in hell

My stomach thinks it's throat's cut: I am very hungry

Nerd: intellectually obsessive, socially impaired

Not the full shillin': useless individual

Nincompoop: unwise idiot

One over the eight: inebriated

Ogham: an ancient script

Otherworld: paradise inhabited by souls of dead

Pattern Day: Catholic custom of repeating a set of prayers while walking in a set way round a shrine or holy place

Put the cat among the pigeons: cause trouble

Quare: very

Quit yer moaning: stop complaining

Quit yer codding: stop joking

Rain coming down in stair rods: very heavy rain

Ramscallion: rascal

Real wee cracker: very attractive girl

Rounds: set of movements performed while saying prayers

Shee: fairies

Snifter: alcoholic drink

Skinful: inebriated

Shuck: shocked. It can also mean a ditch, a stream. In Ireland, Britain can be referred to as 'across the shuck': that is, across the Irish Sea

Smithereens: broken into pieces

Snick: individual worthy of praise, very clever

Some pup: outstanding individual

Stickin' out: excellent

Sleeked: sneaky individual, cannot be trusted, underhand

Snatters: phlegm from a runny nose

Smasher: very attractive individual

Scaredy custard: coward

Spuds: potatoes

Shove it up you sideways: that was a very annoying statement I intend to ignore

Thon: that

Talking through yer left ear: talking nonsense

Thanks a bucket: thank you very much

Whippersnapper: young person with a tendency to be bold

Wheeker: very good, excellent, fantastic

Wheen: a lot of, numerous

Whoppers: untruths, lies

What gives: what is going on?

Yon: that

Yellow hill: a hill associated with the wee folk (fairies)

You'd have sardines for dinner and say ye'd had fish: you are pretentious

Ye must crack the nut before ye can eat the kernel: difficulties come before rewards

Yer bum's out the door: that is nonsense

Ye're no the full whack: you are unwise

Yellow streak up the centre of yer back: cowardly

Ye're chicken: you are easily scared

Yer head's a marley: you're unwise, crazy

You and what army: you would need the help of an army to get the better of me

BIBLIOGRAPHY

Campbell, J.J., *Legends of Ireland* (Batsworth Ltd, 1995)

Carr, Peter, *The Big Wind* (The White Row Press, 1991)

Colum, Padraic (ed.), *A Treasury of Irish Folklore* (Wings Books, 1992)

Crawford, Michael G., *Legendary Stories of Carlingford Lough District* (W.G Havern, 1965)

Cunningham, Noreen and McGinn, Pat, *The Gap of the North* (O'Brien Press, 2001)

Danagher, Kevin, *The Year in Ireland: Irish Calendar Customs* (Mercier Press and Irish Books and Media, 1972)

Gimbutas, Marija, *The Language of the Goddess* (Harper Collins, 1991)

Gimbutas, Marija, *The Living Goddesses* (University of California Press, 2001)

Graves, Alfred Perceval, *The Irish Fairy Book* (Philip Allan & Co. Ltd, 1935)

Gregory, Lady, *Cuchulain of Muirthemne* (Colin Smythe, Gerrads Cross, 1902)

Hall, Mr and Mrs S.C., *Ireland: Its Scenery, Character and History,* Vol. 2. (Hall, Virtue and Co., 1841)

Mallory, J.P. (ed.), *Aspects of The Táin* (December Publications, 1992)

Mallory, J.P., and Stockman, G. (eds), Ulidia: Proceedings of the First International Conference on the Ulster Cycle of Tales (Belfast and Emain Macha, 8–12 April 1994)

McDonnell, Hector, *Holy Hills & Pagan Places of Ireland* (Wooden Books, 2008)

McDonnell, Hector, *St Patrick, His Life and Legend* (Wooden Books, 2007)

Murphy, Anthony, *Newgrange* (The Liffey Press, 2012)

O'Rahilly, Cecile, ed., 'Táin Bó Cúailnge', *Book of Leinster* (Dublin Institute of Advanced Studies, 1984)

O'Rahilly, Cecile, ed., *Táin Bó Cúailnge*, Recension I (Dublin Institute of Advanced Studies, 1976)

Scott, Michael, *Irish Folk and Fairy Tales* (Sphere Books Ltd, 1989)

Stephens, James, *The Crock of Gold* (Macmillan & Co., 1912)

Simms, George Otto, *Saint Patrick* (O'Brien Press, 1991)

Woods, Kevin J., *The Last Leprechauns of Ireland* (Original Writing Ltd., 2013)

Wright, Brian, *Brigid: Goddess, Druidess and Saint* (The History Press, 2009)

Yeats, W.B. (ed.), *Irish Fairy and Folk Tales* (Walter Scott Ltd, 1888)